Kenny hates getting milked — the process where Doc Anthony eases his snake's fangs through a thin lid covering a cup in order to collect his venom. Still, he knows it's a necessary evil if he expects to live in a shifter pod. The doc needs it so he can always have anti-venom on hand, and since he used his last vial to save a human Kenny had bitten, he needs to make more.

Imagine Kenny's surprise when, as Doc Anthony sinks his fangs through the paper, an amazing scent teases his senses. The distraction causes him to pop his head up, and he nearly stabs a fang into the doc. In the doc's shock, he fumbles Kenny's snake form, dropping him to the counter.

A set of hands Kenny doesn't recognize grabs him. He struggles for an instant until he catches his new holder's scent. Stilling, Kenny realizes the big human holding him with a firm and confident hand is his mate. He listens for a moment, learning the man is Renaldo Martinez, and he's a snake enthusiast.

When Kenny shifts, revealing what he is and declaring their connection — that Renaldo is the other half of his soul — will he be able to convince his human to be just as enamored with him in human form?

Submerging with a Sea Snake
Copyright © 2022 Charlie Richards
ISBN: 978-1-4874-3661-2
Cover art by Angela Waters

Published by eXtasy Books Inc

Look for us online at:
www.eXtasybooks.com

Submerging with a Sea Snake

Beneath Aquatica's Waves Thirteen

By

Charlie Richards

DEDICATION

*The beautiful thing about learning is that no one can take it away
from you.*
~BB King

CHAPTER ONE

"Well, I sorta feel like I need a shower after dealing with that guy," Renaldo Martinez drawled as he reentered the conference room.

Elioch Parkinson lifted his attention from the brief offered by Ramone Windervine. "He did remind me of a greasy snake oil salesman," he mused, frowning. After another glance at the brief before pushing it away from him, the lanky, dark-skinned male rose from the table. "I have no idea how he thought you'd go for this horse shit."

The fact that Elioch cussed told Renaldo exactly how offended he was. His best friend of nearly twenty-five years was usually the most mild-mannered of men. In fact, that was how Renaldo had originally met him while in grade school.

Renaldo had spotted Elioch being bullied by a trio of jerks on the playground during recess in sixth grade. While Renaldo had sprouted like a weed even before puberty, making him bigger than most, his mother had instilled in him a sense of fairness that hadn't allowed him to stand by. Elioch, on the other hand, was the quintessential geek — skinny and nerdy with glasses.

After sending the bullies on their way, Renaldo and Elioch had become fast friends. Good thing, too, because they'd ended up helping each other make their way through school. Elioch was a wiz with anything electronic, not to mention the sciences. Renaldo helped coach his friend through social interactions, keeping him off the bully radar.

The fact that Renaldo ended up six-foot-three of pure muscle and everyone knew that Elioch was his best friend had probably helped, too.

They'd even gone into business together. Right after college, Renaldo became the face of a small company offering state-of-the-art electronics chips for the motherboards in computers. The technology had been an instant success, but instead of selling as a start-up and making hundreds of thousands, they'd decided to get a loan and build on it themselves.

The choice had paid off in spades — or millions — and two years prior, Renaldo had convinced Elioch to become more hands-on in the business. His buddy had officially gone on record as the head of their research and development department, which currently boasted six employees.

"How he thought *we'd* go for this horse shit," Renaldo teased, gently correcting his friend, reminding him that he had just as much of a voice in their company's decisions. His friend still suffered from self-esteem issues, and Renaldo refused to ever think he would take advantage of him. "And this isn't the first time he's made a proposal to buy us out, even if he did pretty this offer up by making it sound like a merger." Renaldo lifted his fingers and made air quotes.

Elioch tilted his head to the side, furrowing his black brows behind his brown-rimmed glasses. "Really? How come I don't remember that?"

"It was three years ago, and you hadn't become quite as involved in the management aspects, yet," Renaldo explained, picking up his own copy of Ramone's offer. "You were immersed in the development of that laser guidance chip, so I'm not surprised you don't remember." Grinning, Renaldo thought fondly of how his friend always lost himself in his research. If it was an important meeting, he made a point of swinging by Elioch's office — or workroom — to get him with plenty of time to spare. "Plus, I think I only mentioned it in passing. I knew it wasn't something you would be the least bit interested in. Even working on the guidance chip, you were already mentally immersed in that contract for nanite enhancement we'd just won."

Upon the word *nanites*, Elioch's black eyes lit up. "That was so much fun." He grinned broadly, obviously thinking of the work he'd put in. "It was so easy, too. I don't know why their own engineers hadn't spotted the problem right away. All they had to do was—"

"Whoa there, Eli." Renaldo lifted his free hand, hoping to stop his buddy's diatribe into complex electronics that he couldn't hope to understand. When doing proposals, he had to make copious notes when Elioch described things to him. "Anyway, give me that copy. I'll file mine, have yours recycled, and write up a polite *thank you but no thank you* letter."

Elioch nodded, handing over the packet. "You know, with the way they worded what would happen to the human resources and administration departments, they were pretty much telling you that *you'd* be out of a job."

Renaldo barked a laugh as he nodded. "They did, didn't they." He shook his head as he led the way out of the conference room. "Whoever wrote this isn't the brightest bulb in the box."

Upon hearing Elioch's snickers, Renaldo smirked.

Ramone had briefly brushed over the fact that upon merging with *Perisource Enterprises*, their own company's human resources, administration, accounting, and marketing departments would be made redundant. Renaldo had asked if openings were available to accommodate their people, and Ramone had hedged that there were a few. Then he'd hurried to say that if there weren't any openings that fit their skills, they would be given a generous severance package.

Considering Renaldo felt as if all his employees—even the

six other people that made up those departments — were family, he had no intention of dumping them on the street, even with a *generous severance package*. After all, once an employee had been with the company for six months, they were given the option of investing in the company. Renaldo had found that, if an employee did that, they would have a personal stake in how well the company did.

Currently, the majority of their company's stock was owned by himself and Elioch. The remaining twenty percent was held in various percentages by their twenty-two employees. No way would he force out nearly a quarter of his people.

Large corporations like *Perisource Enterprises* just didn't understand that mentality.

"It's Friday, and once I'm done with this *no thanks* letter, I'm heading out early," Renaldo reminded Elioch. "You need anything before I go?"

Elioch shook his head as he hit the *up* button, calling for the elevator car. "No." As he waited, he peered at Renaldo. "I know you told me, but where are you going again?" Then his buddy grinned cheekily. "Got a hot date with one of your fuck buddies?"

Grinning broadly, Renaldo shook his head as he let out a chuckle. "No, something even better."

His friend knew that he had a series of women — and a couple of men — that he hooked up with when the itch set in. While his mother harped on him about settling down, he didn't consider himself ready. His work wasn't his life by any means, and he enjoyed a myriad of physical activities every weekend — from camping to fishing to surfing and everything in between. He'd learned the importance of downtime from watching his father destroy their homelife — which culminated in his parents divorcing when he was fourteen — not to mention the man's health when his father hit forty-seven. Too many hours at the office, as well as a horrific diet and not enough downtime, ended in the man suffering a massive heart attack.

Renaldo refused to let that happen to himself, but that didn't mean he had any desire to try to figure out how to fit someone else's needs into his schedule.

Besides, I'm only thirty-eight, and people are living longer. I have time.

"What's better than sex?" Elioch asked.

Spoken like a geek who doesn't get any.

Smiling fondly at Elioch, Renaldo thought of the few times he'd tried to set his buddy up for a good time. They'd all been mitigated disasters, so he didn't do that anymore.

"Do you remember Deckart Waldorf from marketing?" Renaldo asked. If the employee hadn't worked in the research and development department, Elioch might not recall him.

Elioch squinted for a second, obviously in thought. "Oh, that cute slender guy with the dick boyfriend?"

Renaldo nodded. "Yeah. Well, he has a new boyfriend now, and he's working at *World of Aquatica*. He arranged for me to get a backstage tour." Excited anticipation filled him as he thought about what was to come. "I even get to see them milk a sea snake. How cool is that?"

Even as Elioch curled his lip in obvious distaste, he stuck out his arm to catch the elevator before the door could close. "Uh, only you would think that's cool," he muttered.

Knowing Elioch wasn't a fan of, well, reptiles in general, Renaldo just shrugged. "What can I say? I find them fascinating." He took a step backward and waved. "If you don't need anything, I'll talk to you on Monday."

Elioch nodded in an absent manner as he stepped into the elevator car. "Yeah, have a good weekend." His expression had turned vacant, telling Renaldo that he was probably already thinking about whatever project he was working on.

As the doors slid shut, Renaldo grinned and hurried to his office, ready to finish up his duties for the day so his weekend could start.

Kenny mentally grumbled. He hated this aspect of living in a shifter pod. Getting milked while in snake form completely sucked.

Such indignity.

Still, Kenny really did love his life. He enjoyed so many luxuries that he never before would have been able to experience. Taking Alpha Kaiser Roush up on his offer to join his pod and work at their aquatic marine park was the best decision he'd ever made.

With that in mind, Kenny didn't protest when Enforcer Craeg called him and told him that Doctor Anthony was prepping for him. He'd known the doc wanted to get the milking done at some point that afternoon, so he'd left his day open. Kenny hadn't even gone to the marine park to troll for a hookup.

Oddly enough, there were plenty of single people who frequented the park who were willing to share in a bit of fun in order to get a behind-the-scenes experience. All Kenny had to do was wear a security uniform and watch for someone checking him out. As long as the scent of the human was right, he didn't mind if it was a man or a woman.

Alpha Kaiser, being a colossal squid shifter, understood a paranormal's high sex drive. When he'd built the place, he'd even incorporated a number of nooks and crannies into the place for just such activities. As long as everyone was discreet, they cleaned up after themselves, and the activity was consensual, Alpha Kaiser didn't give a shit who used what areas.

Maybe after I get this done, I'll find a hot young thing to relieve the stress created by this.

Seeing as this was being done in animal form, Kenny headed to the medical facility for animals. While many of the animals viewed in the tanks and aquariums were shifters, there were just as many of the non-shifter variety, too. This facility was where Enforcer Craeg had told him to meet the doc.

While Kenny found it odd, he didn't question it. He figured as he was already within the bowels of the marine park, he would be that much closer to the main grounds. Kenny could slip out a side door and start trolling for a little fun.

After a ten-minute stroll, Kenny arrived at the animal medical wing. There were several aquatic animals in large aquariums, each being monitored for various things. A huge saltwater crocodile lounged docilely in a secure area.

"Damn." Kenny pointed at it, finding Doctor Anthony standing at a prep table. "What happened to Edgar?"

Doctor Anthony glanced his way, then at Edgar the crocodile. "According to the cameras, some jerk fed him a burger and fries from the Cantina." Scowling, he growled softly as he added, "Normally, that wouldn't bother the boy, but another camera angle showed that he sprinkled something on the fries, and I can assure you it wasn't ketchup."

"Damn." Shock filled Kenny. "Someone tried to poison Edgar?"

Some people are just too horrible to let live.

"Seems that way," Doctor Anthony confirmed, his cheeks darkening as the scent of his anger began perfuming the air. "Preliminary tests showed arsenic."

It was Kenny's turn to growl. "Please tell me that Ovram is using facial recognition to track down the asshole."

Doctor Anthony's smile turned feral as he focused on Kenny. "The guy's already in custody."

Even seeing the doc's rather creepy smile, relief filled Kenny. "Good." He could never understand why anyone abused an animal . . . for any reason. Rubbing his palms over his opposite upper arms, Kenny looked over the items on the table and spotted the cup with the thin plastic covering. "Well, let's get this over with. How much do you need?"

"Mmmm," the doc mused, staring at the cup. "If you can give me three milliliters, I bet I can make four or five injections from it."

Kenny nodded. "Good. Then I won't have to do this again for a few decades," he quipped with a smirk as he reached for the hem of his polo shirt.

"My thoughts exactly," Doctor Anthony agreed. With a smile of understanding, he added, "I know you don't like this process, but we appreciate your willingness to do it."

Nodding once more, Kenny didn't bother responding. He quickly folded his shirt before placing it on a nearby chair. After he kicked off his sandals, his shorts followed his shirt.

Unmindful of his nudity, Kenny hopped onto the metal table. He hissed softly upon feeling the cold on his ass. Even as he mentally winced at how that would translate to his cold-blooded form, Kenny began to shift anyway.

As usual, Kenny's body transitioned swiftly. His legs and arms merged with his narrowing frame. His olive-toned skin rippled as scales formed in bands of brownish-black and creamy white. He closed his eyes as his head morphed, the push and pull a familiar sensation.

Then Kenny's eyelids were gone, and he viewed the world in a variety of hues of reds, yellows, and grays. He spotted Doctor Anthony moving toward him, his lean, toned body shape familiar to him. Kenny lay still as the doc reached for him.

As a sea snake, Kenny had very little ability to move while on land. His long, lean body and tail shaped similar to an oar just weren't designed for it. The only reason he could at all was because he still maintained his human brain. He recalled how earth snakes used their muscles, allowing him a limited range of motion.

Kenny didn't try to utilize that knowledge, though. Instead, he accepted Doctor Anthony's handling. He was lifted into the air, most of his seven-foot body cradled in one hand. Kenny felt the doc's other hand behind his head, urging him to open his mouth.

Obliging, Kenny couldn't resist flicking out his tongue and scenting the world around him. To his surprise, something . . . amazing . . . tickled his senses. Jolting in shock, Kenny whipped his head around, scenting again, trying to discern direction.

"Gee-zus!" Doctor Anthony cried in obvious surprise.

The hands cradling him loosened, and Kenny felt himself tumbling back to the metal trolley.

When Kenny hit the hard surface, he lay there in shock for a few seconds. Then the exquisite flavor registered again, and his desire to find the source coursed through him. Bunching his muscles, Kenny slithered to the left.

A pair of large hands suddenly pinned him to the surface of the trolley. Fingers gripped behind his head in a surprisingly gentle hold as the other hand held him halfway down. Even still, being held by a stranger, Kenny hissed in agitation.

Except, that was when the stranger's scent registered, and he realized the human was the source of the delicious aroma.

Holy shit! He's my mate!

CHAPTER TWO

Acting on instinct upon seeing the venomous snake fall to the metal table, Renaldo lunged forward and gripped it. He'd handled snakes in the past, although this was the first time they'd been of the poisonous kind while technically unsupervised. Still, he remembered his training and gripped behind the snake's head in a firm hold. Renaldo rested his other palm over the creature's back, and he pinned it in place.

For several seconds, the snake writhed, trying to get away. Then, to his surprise, it just . . . stopped. Although, it did flick out its forked tongue repeatedly.

"Damn it, Kenny," the man whom Deckart had referred to as Doc Anthony grumbled, frowning at the snake. "What the hell were you thinking?"

Renaldo arched one brow as he glanced between the lean doctor and the snake in his grip. "Uh, I'm Renaldo. Renaldo Martinez," he told him, figuring he needed to explain. "I'd never seen a milking, but I've had training in handling snakes."

Doctor Anthony cleared his throat as he glanced from Renaldo to the snake and back again. "Uh, no, I was talking to —" He paused and shook his head. Glancing over Renaldo's shoulder, he used a palm to rub the back of his neck. "Hey, um, Craeg. Deckart," he seemed to greet uncertainly. "What's, uh —" Doctor Anthony used a hand to wave toward Renaldo.

"Special permission from Beta William," Craeg replied, confusing Renaldo further. He cleared his throat as the big,

Scottish-accented man shifted from foot to foot. "Didna plan to interrupt."

Nodding slowly, Doctor Anthony slowly bent at the waist, eyeing the snake—Kenny, perhaps. "No, the snake is Kenny," he stated softly, confirming Renaldo's suspicion. "He seems calm enough now. Not sure what the hell set him off." Doctor Anthony began reaching toward the snake. "I'll take him off your hands there, Renaldo. Gotta finish milking him."

Renaldo nodded slowly as he waited for Anthony to take the snake from his grip. Except, when the doc's hands were within a few inches of the snake's body, it opened its mouth in an angry-sounding hiss. The doc eased back, lifting his hands, palms out a little.

"Okaaaaay," Doctor Anthony mused, glancing between them. "Seems Kenny's calm in your hands." His brows were furrowed, and he exchanged a look with Craeg before refocusing on Renaldo. "Well, you wanna learn how to milk a snake, Renaldo?"

Excitement flooded Renaldo as did nerves in equal measure. "Uh, yeah." He grinned broadly as he glanced from the cup to the snake and back again. "I'd love to."

Doctor Anthony glanced at Craeg again, who lifted one big shoulder in a half-shrug. Then the doc eyed the snake. "You better damn well behave, Kenny."

Renaldo was sure he did *not* actually see the snake nod just a smidge, but it certainly looked like it.

After clearing his throat, Doctor Anthony walked through what he needed to do, and Renaldo listened carefully. He had to admit, it didn't sound too difficult. Keeping a firm grip behind the snake's head, Renaldo held the creature's body in his other hand. He lifted the snake carefully before easing the creature's fangs through the thin plastic covering the cup.

As if Kenny knew exactly what was going on, the snake instantly released a large quantity of venom into the cup.

"That'll do it," Doctor Anthony stated, eyeing the cup. "Now, carefully ease him free." He took a couple of steps backward and glanced around the room. "I'll, uh, I'll just get you a tub to put him in."

Renaldo nodded as he carefully eased the snake's teeth from the plastic. The beast immediately closed its mouth. As the doc moved away, Renaldo took a moment to just admire the beast in his hands.

The snake had to be around seven feet in length, making it the largest one he'd ever held outside of a python. It had bands of brownish-black offset with slightly off-white ones. The head was mostly black with a single white band around its snout. It had a slightly compressed body and paddle-like tail, reminiscent of an eel.

To Renaldo's surprise, when he looked into the creature's black eyes, he thought there appeared to be a gleam of intelligence within them.

Noticing Doctor Anthony's approach, Renaldo tore his gaze away from the animal. He spotted the plastic bin and found himself somewhat disappointed that his time with the exotic creature was coming to an end.

Maybe I can come back and learn more about it . . . and maybe some others.

Renaldo could hope, anyway.

Just as Renaldo began easing the snake into the plastic tub, the body within his grip gave a hard shudder. The bones felt as if they slid beneath his palms. Shocked, Renaldo couldn't help but yank his hands away, dropping it.

The snake landed in the bin for all of two seconds before Doctor Anthony cussed and released it. The tub crashed to the floor, and the snake slid across the hard tile.

Except, by then, it didn't look like a snake anymore.

Renaldo gaped, backing one step, then two, as before his eyes, the snake turned into something . . . else. Its body expanded and grew. The scales receded, leaving behind smooth olive-toned skin. Arms and legs formed, full of leanly toned muscle definition.

"Just breathe, man," Craeg urged.

Renaldo nodded even as he tried to obey. The spots dancing before his eyes told him he really needed to do just that. He even felt the large security guard's firm grip on his upper arm, holding him steady.

"There ya go," Craeg rumbled. "Everythin' will be fine." The man narrowed his deep green eyes as he eyed what used to be a snake. "I'ma certain Kenny has a damn good reason for changin' before ya."

"I do." The creature that had once been a snake spoke in a soft tenor. "Renaldo is my mate."

"Well, that explains a lot," Doctor Anthony commented dryly. "Kenny, pull on your shorts."

The snake—Kenny, who was not a snake anymore—took the shorts from the doc's grip. Even as he continued to stare right at Renaldo with piercing black eyes, he pulled them on. Still, that left a lot of smooth skin on display.

To Renaldo's surprise, he found his body responding to the provocative sight before him. The guy stood maybe five-foot-ten and had a lean muscular frame. He would fit perfectly against Renaldo's bigger bulk. His ear-length, wavy-black hair would be just right to bury his fingers into so he could hold his head steady while plundering the man's mouth with his tongue.

Renaldo shook his head once, trying to clear his suddenly lustful thoughts. Unable to help himself, he blurted, "Holy shit. What the hell is going on?"

Kenny could scent Renaldo's arousal, and it was sending his own need soaring. Never in his life could he recall wanting a man so much as he did the large, broad-shouldered human before him. His mate had to stand six-foot-three and sported miles of muscles. The form-fitting polo shirt he wore show-cased a very lovely six-pack that Kenny couldn't wait to trace with his tongue.

"Kenny," Enforcer Craeg rumbled. "Renaldo's yer mate, eh?"

Jerking a nod, Kenny couldn't tear his gaze away from the gorgeous specimen of maleness before him. Fate had defi-nitely blessed him with a sturdy human who he hoped would easily be able to keep up with his lustful appetites. Rarely could Kenny truly let go while having sex, but he just knew Renaldo would enjoy sweat-inducing, energetic bed-play.

"Kenny!"

Upon hearing Craeg's bark, Kenny yanked his gaze to the enforcer. To his surprise, he found the whale shifter smirking at him. The Scottish enforcer rolled his eyes before arching one pointedly.

"Yes," Kenny confirmed, recalling the enforcer's question. Evidently, he needed a verbal confirmation. Maybe he wanted to scent him. Either way, Kenny would never deny the gift Fate was handing him. "Yes," Kenny repeated, even more firmly. "Renaldo is my mate."

Then Kenny couldn't help but return his attention back to the clearly shell-shocked human in question.

Right. I shifted in front of my completely unknowing mate.
Oops.

Lifting his hands in placation, Kenny took a step toward Renaldo. He even held out his hand, although he wanted far more than just a hand shake.

"I'm so sorry for shocking you, Renaldo," Kenny began, doing his best to keep his voice soothing as he eased one step closer, then another. "Unfortunately, it's never a good time to reveal shifters to a human, but I needed you to know."

Renaldo slipped out a pink tongue, licking the bottom of his full lips.

Kenny couldn't help focusing on the bit of gleam left behind and wondering what it would taste like.

"Um, I-I'm so confused," Renaldo mumbled, although he did take Kenny's hand.

He seemed to do it more as a reflex action because of Kenny's outstretched hand, but that was okay. The move still sent a wonderful zing of tingles up Kenny's arm. It even caused the hairs there to stand on end and his skin to goose bump.

Then Renaldo tugged his hand free while sucking in a harsh gasp. He backed up a step as his attention skittered around the others in the room. Finally, he settled on Deckart, who stood a little ways back and wore a wide-eyed, surprised expression.

"Did you—" Renaldo shook his head once, then squinted at him. "You look just as shocked." The larger man began sidling toward him, casting a look around the room again, this one ripe with wariness. "Maybe we should get out of here," Renaldo muttered, frowning. "We can, uhhhh, talk to your friends another time."

That comment seemed to pull Deckart out of . . . whatever. "Oh, no. No!" he cried. He began to reach out, as if intending to grip Renaldo's hand, but then he must have thought better of it. Deckart kept his hands up, palms out, in obvious placation. "Seeing Kenny shift isn't why I was in shock." Then he rolled his eyes and muttered, "Yes, okay. Yes, it shocked me. I've only seen Rawlins shift, but we're totally safe." He focused an earnest expression on Renaldo. "Please, Mister Martinez. I promise we're safe, and everything is okay." Flapping a hand in an absent manner, Deckart assured, "These guys would never hurt us . . . ever."

While Kenny appreciated the vote of confidence, he hated that his mate had moved away from him. He also didn't like the disbelief he scented from him or that filled the tone of his voice.

"You're certain?" Renaldo glanced around the room once more, his gaze assessing, almost as if he were looking for escape routes. "Because I'm pretty sure shit like this is supposed to be kept a secret." Renaldo scrubbed a hand through his short hair. "Shit. Did I just say that out loud?"

"Beta William, we have a ... situation," Enforcer Craeg stated into his phone, drawing Kenny's attention.

With his enhanced shifter hearing, Kenny easily made out the deep tones of the beta's response. "Please tell me Kenny didn't end up biting someone in irritation because he didn't know he was being watched." The beta shifter's deep sigh came through the line before he spoke again, sounding a mixture of frustration mixed with fatigue. "I'm the one who gave permission for Renaldo to view Kenny's milking. I know he's a private person, but I didn't think it would be that big of a deal."

"No, no, Beta," Craeg instantly assured. "Nothing like that. It's, uh ..." Then the big male scoffed and grumbled, "I'm damn jealous because another shifter found his mate, and it wasn't me."

"Uh ... wait." William sounded confused for a few seconds. Then a deep chuckle came through the line. "Wait a minute. Are you saying Renaldo ended up being Kenny's mate?"

Kenny couldn't help but grin as he sidled closer to Craeg and stated, "Yes, Beta." He still couldn't tear his gaze away from his still-wary-looking mate. "Renaldo is my mate. I may have, uh ... shocked the shit out of him, but I just couldn't help myself."

Beta William barked a laugh before saying, "Yeah, it can happen that way." Obviously knowing Kenny could hear him, he added, "You need to bring him round for explanations? Or is he handling it okay?"

Grimacing, Kenny peered into Renaldo's brown eyes that had peered at him with such warmth and interest when he'd been in sea snake form. Now, not so much. Instead, there was nothing but distrust with a side of confusion within their depths.

"Um, not so much," Kenny admitted with a sigh. "Uh, shifting in front of him without warning may not have been the best course of action." Still holding Renaldo's gaze, hoping to convey the depths of his sincerity, he told the beta, "Me and Deckart have assured him that he's safe, but Renaldo is a little . . . freaked out."

"Understandable," William replied. "Bring him to the lounge. I'll be there with John. If all else fails, he'll believe a police captain."

"Thank you, Beta William," Kenny immediately replied, relief filling him. He wasn't certain how the beta intended to have his mate with him on a Friday afternoon—Captain John Casinov—but he appreciated it. "As soon as we can convince him to come, we'll be there."

Then Kenny stepped away from where, at some point, Craeg had put the phone on speaker phone so everyone could hear. "Do you know William Roush?" he asked curiously, as he moved toward Renaldo. Kenny desperately wanted to touch his mate, even if it was just to skim his fingertips down the man's arm.

"Only by reputation," Renaldo admitted softly, his stance remaining tense. "Him and his brother."

"Then you know they're straight-shooters and never do anything without a reason," Doctor Anthony cut in, moving close and holding out Kenny's shirt and sandals to him. "They take care of their own, their family." The doc smirked as he added, "And you just became family by default. You're totally safe with us. Need me to remind you of my Hippocratic Oath?"

Renaldo slowly shook his head. Except, his attention landed on Deckart. "You promise, Deck?"

Deckart grinned broadly. "Oh, this is such a great thing. I'm so happy for you!" Then his expression dimmed a little. "Um, but it is life-changing. You should be prepared for that."

"No, I can't promise that," Renaldo stated, shaking his head, a frown curving his full lips.

After everything had been explained, Kenny couldn't believe Renaldo's refusal to keep their secret. They'd outlined why they hid in plain sight. There were those all over the globe who were persecuted, and if the general human populace knew about them, shifters would be one of them.

Hell, there were already hidden groups that searched for them for experimentation or termination, whichever fit that group's ideals.

"Look, I'm really sorry to have to say this." William leaned forward, cradling his tumbler of whiskey between his palms. It wasn't often the fun-loving beta sported such a serious look, but he pinned it on Renaldo right then. "I can't let you leave until you understand why shifters, and paranormals, need to be kept secret. This isn't a request on a whim."

Renaldo stared into his own tumbler of tequila, pinching his lips into a frown. "Look, it's not like I'm going to go out and put an ad in the paper or something like that." He glanced at Kenny, then focused on William. "I get discretion. I really do. But I can't keep this type of secret from my business partner. He's like a brother to me." After a few seconds of hesitation, where silence filled the room, Renaldo added, "And if I were to suddenly get serious with a guy" — he pinned a speculative look on Kenny — "which is what I understand you're saying is going to happen to us" — then he refocused on William — "then Elioch will wonder what the hell is happening to me."

William's dark brows furrowed as he asked, "You can't just tell him it was love at first sight or some shit?"

Scoffing, Renaldo curled his lip. "I don't believe in love. First sight or otherwise," he declared with a roll of his eyes. "Elioch knows this. What's happening between us" — he indicated between himself and Kenny — "he'll consider that a puzzle." Renaldo's expression grew serious. "And my brother from another mother excels at puzzles. We can't give him one."

William drew in a deep breath as he exchanged a look with John, his own mate.

As they seemed to have a silent deliberation, Kenny could only think one thing.

Well, shit. My mate doesn't believe in love? Why the hell not?

CHAPTER THREE

Letting out a slow breath, Renaldo stood leaning against his vehicle in the parking lot. Only three other vehicles were parked there, and he knew why. The waves were mild at this particular beach today. Those on it were probably in training or there for a picnic or some other beach activity.

If the situation had been anything other than what it was, Renaldo would have found a better place to surf—a place with bigger, more consistent waves. Except, this day was anything but ordinary. In truth, he could still hardly believe the shit he was about to share with his best friend.

Except, I have to.

Renaldo knew anything other than total transparency would just pique Elioch's interest and make his friend question . . . everything.

Wrapped in thought, Renaldo didn't notice until Elioch parked his sedan damn near right on his toes. He snapped his attention to the man behind the wheel and scowled at him. Unfortunately, the look was lost on Elioch because his friend wasn't even looking at him.

Heaving a sigh, Renaldo rolled his eyes. He even noticed that Elioch had parked his car almost perfectly between the lines. Shaking his head, he reached up and began unhooking the pair of surf boards from his *Subaru*'s rack.

Elioch didn't own a surfboard, although the man did know how to surf . . . sort of. His friend knew the mechanics, but he was damn uncoordinated. He couldn't always pull it off.

"Why the hell did you insist on this?" Elioch grumbled as

he stalked around his car and stopped before him. He rested his fists on his hips and glared up at him. "It better be damn good, and no matter what, you totally owe me my favorite pizza, hot wings, and cheesy breadsticks when we're done."

His friend already wore a pair of goggles on his face, and Renaldo knew they were prescription. He couldn't see a whole heck of a lot without them.

Holding out a surf board to Elioch, Renaldo assured, "If it wasn't super important, I wouldn't have insisted."

After all, where can I get Elioch to be a captive audience, away from computers and other electronic distractions, if not out in the ocean . . . and I don't have a boat.

Not that my buddy fishes.

"Come on," Renaldo urged before Elioch could ask any more questions. He turned and started toward the stairs leading to the beach. Pivoting to walk backward, he stated, "Let's check out a wave or two. Then I'll tell you everything and answer all your questions."

Furrowing his black brows, Elioch started after him, clutching the surf board under his arm.

Renaldo appreciated that Elioch didn't immediately start peppering him with questions. Usually, his friend was like a hound on a trail. If Elioch recognized an issue with Renaldo, he would pester him until he shared whatever the issue was.

It had happened in the past. Over the years, Renaldo had been able to keep very few secrets from the man. He knew if he embraced all the changes to his life that meeting Kenny — and incidentally, bonding with him — would cause, Elioch would notice and ask question after question.

Walking away and entering waves that made it difficult to shout at each other gave Renaldo just a little more time to figure out how to share . . . everything. He knew Elioch's analytical mind would rebel against the idea at first. Having shared that with the shifters, William had assured him that they would have a few people on hand, scattered about, just in case the worst happened, and Elioch tried to call the men in the white coats on Renaldo.

God, I can't believe that I believe all this shit, but I saw it with my own two eyes.

Never would have thought such things existed.

Such sexy handsome men who turn into fascinating snakes.

They told me that Kenny would want to do whatever would please me, and he even let me explore his snake. He's venomous. Holding him had been such a rush. I could —

"Let's get this over with," Elioch muttered, bumping his shoulder against his upper arm. He narrowed his dark eyes at Renaldo as he stated, "Let's hit a few waves. I'll fall on my ass each time. Then you can tell me what has your panties in a twist."

Grimacing, Renaldo mumbled, "Deal."

Renaldo knew he shouldn't be dwelling on how — after explanation time had ended — he'd gotten to swim with Kenny's snake in an underground grotto, anyway. Those memories were too distracting. While Renaldo hadn't given in to his desire to touch Kenny after he'd gotten naked and before he'd shifted into his snake form, his fingers had twitched with his desire to explore all his smooth skin.

No way do I want to try to surf with a boner.

Instead, Renaldo forced his thoughts to the matter at hand.

Twenty minutes later, Renaldo paddled slowly beside Elioch. They were a good seventy-plus feet from shore. The waves were even smaller than when they'd first started, and he knew it really was time to quit.

Besides, Elioch was panting softly, obviously struggling. His best friend just wasn't used to such physical activity.

Giving in, Renaldo reached over and tapped Elioch on his upper arm. His friend turned his attention from the incoming waves and focused on him. Something in Renaldo's expression must have caught Elioch's attention, for he slowed his arms and nearly stopped paddling.

For several heartbeats, they bobbed beside each other.

"You met someone," Elioch blurted, his brows furrowing. He narrowed his eyes and cocked his head. "Is that what this is about? After all this time, someone finally caught your attention for more than just a one-night stand or fuck buddy?"

After Renaldo gaped for a couple of seconds, a wave splashed into his mouth. He choked and coughed for a moment, catching his breath. Focusing on Elioch once more, he found his buddy waiting patiently, and he even sported an amused expression.

"That's what you're guessing?" Renaldo couldn't help how incredulous he sounded, even with his voice hoarse from hacking. "Where the hell did that come from?"

Elioch scoffed as he rolled his eyes. He even grinned cheekily at Renaldo . . . until a wave made him focus on the ocean and keeping upright. When he returned his attention to Renaldo, a frown curved his brows.

"Come on, Ren," Elioch stated, shaking his head. "I know I'm a little oblivious at times, but think about it. You always talk about your fuck buddies, but you haven't mentioned them in months." After a glance at the waves again to correct his balance, he continued, "Then you leave work early on a Friday, which is rare." Elioch balanced on his elbows and began ticking off his points on his fingers. "Now, on a Saturday, you insist on taking me surfing at a beginner's training ground. You must be bored as hell, which means you're ruminating on something and trying to figure out how to tell me." Shrugging again, Elioch rested his palms back on his board. "Therefore, a major change. It's not work because you wouldn't have this much trouble talking about it. It's not your mom getting sick because you would have told me that immediately." His friend pinned a serious look on him, even as they bobbed on the ocean. "That means . . . a girl. So." Elioch shrugged again. "Spill. Why are you so worked up about this?" Then his eyes widened. "Please don't tell me she lives in another state, and you're leaving me."

Of all the conclusions that Renaldo had guessed Elioch would draw, that had never even been a blip on his radar.

"No!" Renaldo cried, shaking his head emphatically. "I'd never leave you." Waving his hand between them, he splashed droplets between them. "You and me, we're bros from another mother, man. Inseparable fraternal twins."

To Renaldo's relief, he watched the tension in Elioch's slim shoulders ease. "Okay." Then his buddy scowled at him. "So? What gives, man? Stop freaking me out and just tell me."

Realizing he wouldn't have a better opening, Renaldo glanced around to make certain no one was near, but they were almost alone on the waves. Still, he paddled a little closer before admitting, "Okay, so . . . there is someone." When Renaldo saw Elioch's brown eyes widen behind his goggles, he quickly added, "Or, maybe you'd call him a some-*thing*." He frowned and shook his head. "No. That's wrong. Definitely a some*one*."

"Uh, what?"

Renaldo refocused on Elioch and discovered his buddy was staring at him as if he had two heads. After another glance around, he blew out a sharp breath before asking, "You remember I'm bisexual, right?"

Elioch curled his lip as he waved a hand. "It's not the *him* part I'm confused about. What the hell do you mean by some-*thing*?"

Deciding he had no choice but to take the plunge, Renaldo began explaining about shifters and paranormals and *World of Aquatica*.

As Renaldo watched Elioch continue to stare at him in clear disbelief, he finally declared, "And I can prove it all to you beyond any shadow of a doubt."

Finally, Elioch curled his lip, his amusement clear. "Definitive proof?"

"Yes," Renaldo confirmed. Then he quickly added, "But I already sort of promised you'd keep their secret . . . just like I will."

"Keep the existence of shape-shifters a secret? Are you insane?" Elioch cried, staring at him in shock. "That'd be the greatest revelation since man walked on the moon! If it's true, we can't keep it a secret."

Well, shit.

Swimming below Renaldo and his friend where they bobbed on surf boards, Kenny listened to his mate explain shifters and paranormals to his buddy. At first, he preened when his human claimed that there was a special guy that could end up in his life.

No could about it. I will.

Then Kenny overheard Elioch's excitement about sharing their discovery.

Oh, gods. What the hell do I do?

Kenny had never run across a situation where he needed to stop a human from sharing their existence. Other than picking them up for tricks, he rarely interacted with them, at all. Hell, even his driver's license was fake, and he'd never truly taken a driving test. While he had learned the skill from another shifter, he rarely used it. It was so much easier to swim everywhere he needed to go.

Plus, now I can order online.

Kenny had come to love online shopping. In his opinion, it was greater than even the space travel that Elioch seemed to be extolling.

Hmmm . . . another great invention. The cell phone.

Swimming away, Kenny did his best to ignore his mate arguing with his buddy. He knew he needed help . . . that meant getting in touch with his pod. Kenny figured he could swim back to *World of Aquatica*, but he feared it would take too long, and they might miss their window.

Spotting an unoccupied towel, bag, and basket near a discreetly located set of rocks, Kenny swiftly swam that way. He paused in the shallows and made the most discreet shift he'd ever accomplished. Rising to his feet, he made certain the water stayed well above his midsection as he thrust his hair over his forehead and rubbed the water out of his eyes.

Kenny panned over the area again, then swam swiftly toward shore. The secluded area remained unoccupied, so he quickly rushed up the beach and grabbed the towel. Uncaring of the sand, Kenny wrapped the fabric around his lower body and knotted it at his waist.

While Kenny's first impulse was to rummage through the bag in search of a phone, he decided against it. He didn't want someone labeling him a thief. A towel covering a naked man could be explained, after all—*I got caught in an undertow, and it tugged off my swim shorts.*

Considering humans were pretty paranoid about nudity, Kenny didn't think anyone would get upset about him *borrowing* their towel to cover his privates.

Striding down the beach, Kenny analyzed those on the beach for a likely target. He spotted a trio of females who were ogling a number of guys playing volleyball nearby. They were whispering and giggling to each other, his sensitive hearing telling him that they were admiring certain attributes, and he knew he had his mark.

Lowering the front of his towel just a smidge to show off his six-pack abdominals, Kenny approached the trio. The brunette spotted him first, and he offered her a warm smile. After she'd nudged the girl on her right and she was looking, too, he gave them a wave.

"Hey, ladies," Kenny greeted, glancing between them.

"I'm real sorry to interrupt, but my phone got dunked by a friend." He indicated the cell phone between two of the women. "You mind if I make a quick call?" He racked his brain for a reason these ladies would understand and quickly came up with, "I need to call an *Uber* so I can get home and grab my car. Gotta head to the phone store to replace it before it closes." With a grimace, Kenny added, "Need it for work on Monday."

"Oh, yeah, here." The brunette on the right immediately grabbed her phone. She tapped the screen a few times, obviously unlocking it. Then she held it out as she offered a flirty smile. "Are you far? I could probably give you a ride."

"That's really nice of you," Kenny replied with a smile, taking the device. "But I couldn't think of inconveniencing you." He took two steps backward as he quickly punched in Head Enforcer Eban's phone number. "I'll make this quick and get out of your hair."

"Who is this?" Eban grumbled into the phone. The great white shark shifter didn't like electronics at the best of times. He probably really didn't appreciate getting a call from some random number.

"Hey, Eban. It's Kenny. Sorry to bother you," Kenny greeted. He didn't even need to fake his apologetic tone. "You got a number to *Uber*?" Turning to face the ocean, he lowered his tone and muttered, "I have a code red at Conton Beach. My mate's buddy isn't taking the reveal too well. Can you schedule a discreet pick-up?"

"Damn it, Kenny," Eban muttered. "Whose number is this?"

"Borrowed a nice lady's phone." Kenny turned and winked at the woman, who blushed and smiled. Returning his attention to the ocean, he sought out the pair still on the surfboards a good seventy yards out. "Just needed an assist, is all."

"There are people already in the area," Eban revealed. "Colton and Waylon are pretending to surf, and Saul is getting some sun."

"Saul?" The jellyfish shifter's name was out of Kenny's mouth before he could help himself. "Really?"

The other pair weren't a surprise. Colton was a seahorse shifter mated with Waylon, a human, and they both loved surfing or anything to do with the beach. Saul, however, was their pod's uber-efficient lawyer, and Kenny couldn't imagine the pale shifter's skin feeling the kiss of the sun.

Eban rumbled softly through the line. "Yep. Take another look around. I'm sure you'll find them." After another heartbeat, he told him, "I'll send a text to Saul and Colton, so they'll be looking for you." Eban's voice sounded softer as he stated, "Graham, how do I text on this damn thing?"

Then the line disconnected, and Kenny didn't bother fighting back a laugh. He knew their pod's head enforcer was engaging the help of his human mate. Graham would help Eban with what the other shifter called new-fangled technology.

Okay. Now I just need to find my fellow shifters.

CHAPTER FOUR

Paddling toward shore, Renaldo wondered what else he could say to curb Elioch's sudden excitement. Never in his wildest dreams would he have imagined this response from his best friend. It seemed that no matter what he said, he couldn't seem to convince his buddy that keeping silent was the best option.

Shit! Why didn't I think of this?

Elioch loved figuring out problems, and evidently, that now included discovering the best way to incorporate the paranormal into the human world. It didn't matter that all Elioch had to go on was Renaldo's word that shifters were real. His best friend trusted him that completely—paranormal beings existed.

Then why can't he believe me when I say that keeping them a secret is the best thing?

Renaldo wasn't certain, and he'd never been in a situation where he needed to curb his buddy's enthusiasm for solving a puzzle. In fact, he figured this had to be the greatest puzzle of them all. How could paranormals be incorporated into the human world without repercussions?

I'm not so certain it's possible.

Recalling Beta William's words, Renaldo knew that the shifter leader didn't think it was possible either.

As Renaldo slipped off his board, sinking his feet into the sandy bottom, he realized he might need some help. He had the beta's number. Except, he wondered if revealing Elioch's intentions would be like turning him over to be held against his will.

After all, they talked about holding me unless I promised not to share their existence with anyone.

Catching Elioch's wide grin as he traipsed up the beach beside him, Renaldo tried to decide on the best course of action.

I have Kenny's phone number, too. Maybe I should call him. After all, as my mate, he'll want me happy, and I wouldn't be happy if my best friend was held.

"Oh, come on," Elioch cajoled, bumping his shoulder into Renaldo's upper arm. "This'll be great! Just you wait."

Renaldo barely held in his groan. "Elioch, I'm really sorry, bud, but I don't think you understand what's at stake here." He kept his voice low. The beach had begun filling up with volleyball players, sunbathers, and parents with their kids. Tipping his head down, Renaldo continued, "Don't you think there's a reason that no one knows about them?"

"But you know, and now I know," Elioch replied logically, not bothering to lower his voice in the least. "You said that if you bond with this Kenny shifter guy, it'll mean big changes to your life, and that's why you needed to tell me." With a grin, he added, "Because I would have figured it out anyway, and if I could figure it out, so can others. We totally need to get ahead of this." Elioch continued to grin as he added, "Plus, we'll end up famous. I bet I can get laid as often as I want then."

Frowning, Renaldo grumbled, "You want to expose their secret so you can get laid?"

Elioch barked a laugh, flashing a smirk his way. "Naw, but you should see the look on your face."

Growling softly, Renaldo shook his head. "Sometimes, your sense of humor sucks."

His buddy was too busy laughing to reply.

"Hey, Renaldo, Elioch," a deep voice called. "Wait up!"

Renaldo paused and turned, Elioch doing the same. Spotting a big black man in board shorts jogging toward him would have worried him had it not been for the wide grin he sported. Plus, his gray eyes twinkled with a friendly gleam.

"Do you know him?" Elioch muttered.

Shaking his head slightly, Renaldo admitted his ignorance.

The man paused before him and held out a hand. "Hey, I'm glad I caught up with ya. I'm Waylon."

Taking Waylon's hand on reflex, Renaldo shook. "Nice to meet you, Waylon," he stated, taking in the man's relaxed stance. "Mind if I ask how you know me?"

"Mutual friend," Waylon replied enigmatically. "Come on. My man Colton is taking our boards to our *Jeep*. I know he'll want to meet you, too."

To Renaldo's surprise, Waylon slung his arms over both their shoulders as if they were best friends. "You're Elioch, right?" He began guiding them both up the beach with his considerable strength. "Heard you were going to be in the know, too."

By the time Waylon finished speaking, they were almost to the parking lot. It suddenly hit Renaldo. This man either knew about shifters or was one.

Evidently, Elioch figured it out, too. "You're one of them?" He practically squealed the words with delight. Pulling away from Waylon, he began almost bouncing on his toes as he continued walking beside them. "What kind? Are there others around here?" Elioch glanced around as if other shifters would suddenly appear and present themselves. "Is there a way to tell if someone is a shifter or vampire instead of a human?"

Waylon scoffed as he shook his head, releasing Renaldo's shoulder. "Now I see what Kenny meant about your buddy not intending to keep our secret," he commented, focusing on him. Then Waylon turned his attention to Elioch. "Sorry to burst your bubble, man, but no. I'm not, and no, you really can't tell. That's the point of hiding in plain sight."

31

"But they shouldn't have to hide," Elioch insisted, frowning. "And I'm gonna figure out a way to change all that. I'm —
"

"Looks like you and your friend are coming with us."

Having been so focused on Elioch and Waylon, Renaldo hadn't even noticed the black SUV-style limousine that had rolled to a stop beside them. He saw the side door was open, revealing the interior. Several people he didn't recognize were seated within . . . and one that he did.

The black-haired man with piercing green eyes in the tailored suit should have held Renaldo's attention. Instead, all he could do was stare at the man with the towel wrapped around his waist.

Kenny.

Desire surged through him as Renaldo passed off his surfboard to Waylon before easing into the vehicle and settling in a seat beside the lean man he'd had a hell of a time resisting the prior day. He spotted the answering gleam in Kenny's dark eyes, and heat surged through Renaldo's veins.

Why the hell didn't I take him up on his obvious advances yesterday?

Except, Renaldo knew the answer to that question — doing anything with Kenny would be taken as acceptance of their connection. Still, as he watched a slightly resistant Elioch climb into the vehicle and sit beside a large black man with a shaved head, Renaldo didn't think he had the strength to walk away from Kenny a second time.

When Kenny rested his hand on Renaldo's shorts-clad thigh, his gut clenched, and he practically sprang a boner right there in front of everyone.

Yep. Definitely not walking away.

The scent of Renaldo's arousal was damn near scrambling Kenny's mind. He squeezed the thick muscle under his palm, enjoying the firm feel of it. Kenny barely resisted sliding his hand down his mate's leg so he could touch his skin.

"Sorry, Kenny," Alpha Kaiser rumbled from where he sat on the back bench seat with his mate, Arthur. A hint of amusement entered his tone as he continued, "We all need to have a talk while we return to *Aquatica*. Then you can whisk your mate away to find the nearest flat surface."

Kenny cleared his throat as he jerked a nod. "Yes, Alpha."

The pair had been returning from a business trip to San Diego, where Arthur still ran his company. Upon hearing of Elioch's response to learning about paranormals, he'd ordered his driver, Westram, to make a detour to the beach. Enforcer Dare was the man sitting across from himself and Renaldo, Elioch beside him, as he'd accompanied the pair as their bodyguard.

Alpha Kaiser turned his attention to Elioch. "So, I understand you have a desire to expose our kind to humans in general, with the goal of us all living in peace and harmony."

Nodding slowly, Elioch eyed Kaiser warily. "I've seen you in the news." He nibbled his bottom lip for a second before adding, "So, you're a shifter? He called you alpha. Does that mean you're the leader?"

Kaiser returned Elioch's nod once. "Yes. I'm the leader of the group of shifters who live and work at *World of Aquatica*." He offered Elioch a small smile that didn't reach his intense green eyes. "That also means that everyone who learns about shifters from any of my people are also my responsibility." His smile dimming, Kaiser added, "That includes you, Elioch. *You* are now my responsibility."

Kenny certainly hadn't considered that when he'd done his part to help convince Beta William to allow Renaldo to share the existence of shifters with Elioch. He'd just wanted his mate happy. If having his best friend be *in the know*, as it were, then Kenny wanted that for him.

Except, Kenny worried that it had ended up being a mistake, considering Elioch's response.

Elioch frowned, his brows furrowing behind his swimming goggles. "What do you mean?"

"It means your actions reflect on me," Alpha Kaiser replied solemnly. "It's my responsibility to make certain all those under my supervision follow the rules. Do you know what the number one rule in the shifter world is?"

Slowly, Elioch shook his head.

Renaldo grimaced. "Secrecy, right?"

Alpha Kaiser peered Renaldo's way and nodded once more. "Indeed. Secrecy. We normally don't tell humans about us unless that human is mated with one of our own." Glancing between Renaldo and Kenny, he told them, "Telling Elioch is a hell of a stretch, and it shouldn't have been done without my permission, and Beta William will be getting an earful."

Arthur patted Kaiser's thigh. "You know your brother has a big heart," he murmured, his expression appearing kind. "He likes making everyone happy."

"Which is why I have to make the hard decisions, at times," Kaiser stated while pinning a loving smile on his mate. As he returned his attention to Kenny, that look was gone to be replaced by a serious one. "You're not even bonded with Renaldo, yet. Elioch shouldn't have been told."

Kenny winced, hunching his shoulders upon hearing the gentle chiding. "I'm sorry, Alpha." He grimaced as he glanced Renaldo's way before meeting his alpha's gaze once more. "I just wanted my mate happy." Clearing his throat, Kenny admitted, "I'd hoped that . . . if Renaldo could keep his best friend, he'd want to bond with me, um, the human me."

"Why do you think I don't want to bond with the human you?" Renaldo cut in, sounding and scenting of his confusion. "You're sexy as fuck. Of course, I want the human you."

"You asked me to shift back into my sea snake before leaving Friday night," Kenny pointed out. "As much as swimming with you while in snake form was fantastic, and I need you to be comfortable with both sides of me, you wanted to spend more time with my snake than with me as a human." Grimacing, Kenny couldn't help but say, "And you didn't touch me when I was a human. Only as a snake. It was . . . almost as if you were more interested in my snake than me as a man." Shaking his head, he added, "Even when I was in human form, my snake was all we talked about."

Kenny felt his cheeks heat the more he spoke. He hadn't intended to air his fears in front of everyone, but he couldn't lie to Renaldo. He'd loved pleasing his mate, swimming with him. Unfortunately, he'd craved a different kind of connection, too.

To Kenny's surprise, Renaldo's cheeks took on a pinkish hue. His human shifted in his seat a little. After a glance around the vehicle's cabin, Renaldo refocused on him.

"I didn't mean to make you feel that way. I've never been in a relationship, so I'm bound to screw up," Renaldo muttered, his brown eyes holding a pleading gleam. Grimacing, he added, "And I find snakes and other reptiles fascinating, so the ability to swim with one such as amazing as you was absolutely mind-blowing, even knowing you're totally cognizant while in animal form."

Before Kenny could come up with a response, Renaldo hurried and added, "But the reason I didn't do much more than touch your arm a time or two was because, if I got my hands on you, I wouldn't have stopped." His brown eyes darkened with lust, and his voice lowered to a soft growl. Renaldo rumbled, "I would have had you kneeling in the sand with my cock up your ass so fucking fast, Kenny. Not touching you was all I could do to control myself."

Kenny sucked in a shocked breath as a hot wave of lust

roared through his system. Sliding his hand down, he reached the hot flesh of his mate's knee. He squeezed as he lifted his free hand and began reaching for Renaldo's jaw, wanting to kiss the man so damn badly.

"I don't mean to be a cock-blocker, Kenny," Alpha Kaiser cut in. "But you need to wait a little longer."

Groaning, Kenny dropped his forehead to Renaldo's shoulder. He breathed deeply, but the fragrance of his mate's arousal filling his nostrils wasn't helping. Feeling Renaldo's arm around him, his hand rubbing up and down Kenny's back, helped him settle a bit, though.

"We'll get to us, Kenny," Renaldo whispered huskily into his ear. "Don't worry."

Nodding, sliding his forehead over Renaldo's bare flesh, Kenny pulled himself together. When he straightened, he offered Alpha Kaiser a small smile. "Sorry, Alpha."

Alpha Kaiser smirked. "As am I." Then he returned his attention to Elioch. "So, back to you, Elioch. Now you know our number one rule. Will you keep our secret?"

"But you shouldn't have to hide," Elioch countered, speaking impassionedly. "You deserve to live your lives without fear of persecution if people found out about you. Let me figure out how to make that happen. I know —"

Lifting his hand, Alpha Kaiser cut in, "Every minority group in existence has been persecuted at one time. Many still are. Some are even being put to death for their differences." He shook his head, his expression hardening. "To think we would be treated any different is rather naive, Elioch."

Kenny saw Elioch's eyes narrow, a mutinous gleam entering their dark depths. The way his jaw clenched as well as the scent of his anger told Kenny more than words that Renaldo's friend didn't want to listen.

Evidently, Alpha Kaiser knew it, too. "For your safety and for the safety of paranormals, you have two options, Elioch."

Elioch crossed his arms over his chest. "What? Agree or die?" he snarked.

"No," Alpha Kaiser countered. "Agree and keep our secret or have your memories of any knowledge of us wiped from your mind."

CHAPTER FIVE

"Would Alpha Kaiser really have Elioch's mind erased?" Renaldo asked softly, concern riding him.

They stood in an elevator car, and it was rising to the third floor. He felt a little bad leaving Elioch with Alpha Kaiser and his people, but he knew his friend wasn't listening to his opinion on the matter. He hoped the shifters could get Elioch to understand the need for secrecy.

"Yes," Kenny confirmed, his voice just as quiet. "If he doesn't, and Elioch starts spreading tales of us, it could draw shifter hunters to us." Tipping his chin up, he focused on Renaldo. "If that happens, Elioch officially becomes a danger to our kind. Alpha Kaiser could be sanctioned by the Shifter Council or even removed from his position, since it happened in his territory, and Elioch's mind would just end up wiped by them." Grimacing, Kenny added, "Unless the hunters get to him first. If Elioch didn't cooperate with them, helping them capture us, they would probably kill him as a sympathizer."

"I'm sorry." Renaldo groaned as he rubbed the back of his neck. "I shouldn't have asked for permission to tell Elioch." As much as he wanted to share this fascinating new world with his best friend, he knew that the situation Elioch now found himself in was his fault. "I should have waited until I had all the facts. I had no idea there were such stringent laws in place." Shaking his head, Renaldo continued, "And the dangers. I had no idea, but I suppose I should have guessed. It's—"

"Hey." Kenny gripped Renaldo's hand and gave it a gentle squeeze. "None of this is your fault." Scoffing, the slender male grimaced. "If anything, it's mine. I should have figured out a way to explain things better. I—"

Renaldo turned and wrapped one arm around Kenny's waist. "None of that from you, either," he muttered as he lowered his head. Cradling Kenny's jaw with his other hand, he stated, "We'll figure out this whole communication thing soon enough."

Just not now.

Besides, there were other ways to communicate.

Pressing his mouth to Kenny's, Renaldo finally gave in to his urge to taste the other man. He found his soon-to-be lover's lips soft and inviting. Renaldo eased his lips apart and teased his tongue along Kenny's seam. Immediately, Kenny opened to him, welcoming him inside, and Renaldo took complete advantage.

Renaldo slipped his tongue into Kenny's mouth, sliding his appendage against the other man's. The shifter's flavor burst across his taste buds, masculine and strong. Groaning with pleasure, Renaldo delved deeper while tightening his hold on Kenny's jaw, allowing him to explore him in earnest.

In the past, Renaldo hadn't been much of a kisser. As he enjoyed Kenny, teasing and nipping, he knew that would change. The way the other man pushed into him, giving as good as he got, caused the hairs on his arms to stand on end. Trickles of heat erupted on his skin and surged through his veins.

Tightening his hold around Kenny's waist, Renaldo began to lift him. He had every intention of lifting the shifter and pressing him against the wall, needing to feel his body all along his own. Renaldo needed pressure on his dick in the worst way.

Except, then a deep voice coughed loudly nearby.

Renaldo lifted his head and snapped his attention to the

left. Spotting a big man lounging in the doorway of the elevator, he realized that at some point, they'd arrived. Renaldo couldn't even remember hearing the door ding or feeling the box stop moving.

The guy had his shoulder pressed against the door, keeping it open. His arms were crossed over his chest, as were his legs at the ankles. He smirked at them, his green eyes dancing with mirth.

"Uh, hi, Kayson," Kenny greeted, sounding a mixture of breathless and gruff. "Sorry for holding up the elevator."

"Oh, I didn't mind too much," Kayson replied with a chuckle. "It was a nice show, after all." Then the blond scoffed as he pushed off the door. "But I figured you wouldn't want a voyeur watching your first time with your mate." Winking, Kayson took a step back, using a hand to keep the doors open. "Congrats, by the way."

"Thanks, Kayson," Kenny replied. He eased back a step, causing Renaldo to loosen his hold a bit. "And thanks for being so decent."

Then Kenny took Renaldo's hand and began leading him out of the elevator and to the left.

"Sure, man," Kayson replied. "Just know how I'd feel if it were me."

Then Kayson stepped into the elevator, and the doors closed behind him.

Kenny stopped before a door and used a keypad to unlock the door. After swinging it open, he led the way inside before closing it behind them. He paused in the small foyer and peered up at Renaldo.

Arousal still swam within the dark depths of Kenny's eyes, but questions did, too.

"What?" Renaldo asked, the throb in his dick making it hard to think.

Kenny scoffed quietly before saying, "Everyone's expecting us to have sex and bond right now."

Renaldo nodded. "I figured as much."

"But is that something you want to do?" Kenny asked, staring intently at him. Before Renaldo could respond, the shifter quickly added, "Yes, I want to bond us, but I don't want you to feel pressured. Like we told you before, it'll mean a number of changes in your life."

Humming, Renaldo glanced around the space again. It appeared to be a pretty standard one-bedroom apartment. He spotted the corner of a bed through one open door and a sink within another, telling him which room was which. The open concept of the rest of the space was done in pleasant blue hues reminiscent of the ocean. There was even a sliding glass door beyond the dining room table, and Renaldo saw a small deck beyond it.

"Do you have any bottled water in the fridge?" Renaldo asked.

"Uh, yeah. You thirsty?" Kenny sounded confused even as he pulled away and headed in that direction.

"I am," Renaldo confirmed, following slowly. "But I also want to take a couple of bottles into the bedroom, too." Seeing Kenny pause where he'd opened the refrigerator, Renaldo pinned him with a heated smile. "I know I'll want some after I'm done fucking you through the mattress."

Kenny groaned softly, his lips parting. His tongue slipped between his lips, wetting the bottom one. He snapped his mouth shut and swallowed so hard his Adam's apple bobbed.

Renaldo even noticed the way Kenny's nostrils flared and his dark eyes dilated. "Ah, you do like the sound of that," he crooned, taking a step toward the bedroom. "Don't you?"

"Yeah," Kenny replied huskily. "Yeah, I do."

Then Kenny reached into the refrigerator with both hands. He came back holding two bottles of water in each. Using his hip, he closed the door and started toward Renaldo.

With narrowed eyes, Kenny stated, "You do know that I'll need to fuck you, too, in order to complete the bond."

Taking a deep breath, Renaldo nodded slowly. He did recall that nugget of information. He also knew he needed to come clean with Kenny.

"I've never been on the receiving end, Kenny," Renaldo admitted gruffly. "I, uh, I've always been a pretty big guy, so it, well . . . never came up."

"But you have been with men?" Kenny questioned, stopping beside him. "Water?"

Renaldo took a pair of bottles, freeing Kenny's left hand. "Yeah. I've been with both."

Tucking one under his arm, Renaldo opened the other. He took his time, drinking deeply. In truth, he really was a bit parched. He hadn't had anything to drink since before surfing with Elioch.

Kenny waited until Renaldo screwed the cap back on before saying, "If you need more time, I can bite you while you fuck me, and we'll start the bond that way." Then his cheeks took on a pinkish hue as he quickly added, "Uh, if you're ready for me to start our bond, I mean."

Renaldo set both bottles on the nightstand to the left of the bed. Returning to Kenny, he took the pair he still carried and set them beside the first set. Then Renaldo took Kenny's hand before sitting on the side of the bed and using his hold to urge the shifter to sit next to him.

Holding Kenny's gaze, Renaldo told him, "I'm willing to bond, but I do have a couple of questions."

Nodding, Kenny squeezed his fingers. "I'll answer anything if possible."

After a few seconds of staring at the hardwood floor to gather his thoughts, Renaldo met Kenny's eyes once more. "People keep telling me that bonding will require a lot of change, and that's okay." Scoffing, he added, "I figure it'll bring a lot of change for you, too, and entering any relationship is going to bring change to the pair."

Kenny nodded again as he pointed out, "There wasn't a question in there."

Renaldo chuckled.

Right.

"Does the shifter always expect the human to move in with them?" Renaldo asked slowly. "Or would you be willing to move in with me, instead?"

Surprise coursing through him, Kenny realized that hadn't been what he'd been expecting. He licked his lips, giving the question the attention it was due. What Renaldo had said was true.

For the most part, the shifter did indeed expect the human to move in with them. There were a couple of reasons for that. The most important one, however, was that the shifter was normally part of a group, and that group watched each other's backs and kept each other safe.

"We do normally have the human move in with the shifter, for safety reasons," Kenny began slowly. Seeing the way Renaldo's brows furrowed, he added, "Do you not want to live here by the ocean?" Rubbing the back of his neck, Kenny admitted, "I'm a sea snake shifter, Renaldo. Being close to the ocean is a bit important for me."

Renaldo blew out a breath even as he nodded. Glancing out the bedroom door, he cocked his head. When he met Kenny's gaze again, Renaldo shook his head, which only confused Kenny.

Fortunately, Renaldo's words explained. "I run a business in town, but I wouldn't mind a forty-five-minute commute." He glanced around the space again. "Except, I also work from home quite a bit. I need an office. Is there, uh . . ." Renaldo stalled and scratched at his ear.

Understanding, Kenny squeezed Renaldo's hand, redrawing his attention. "I live here because I'm single and don't need much space." He grinned as he stated, "There are a few empty cottages dotted around the grounds. There's also larger apartments. Two and three bedrooms. Some shifters start families."

Renaldo blanched, his lips parting as his eyes widened. "Is that something you want to do?"

"Start a family?" Kenny clarified.

When Renaldo nodded, his scent betrayed just how much the idea concerned him.

Kenny chuckled as he shook his head. "Maybe in a hundred years," he teased.

Scoffing, Renaldo smirked at him as his shoulders sagged. "Funny." A second later, he asked, "Wait. How old are you? How old do you get again?"

Considering the information dump humans normally received when learning about shifters, Kenny wasn't surprised that Renaldo hadn't retained it all. "I'm one-hundred-seventeen," he told him. "And shifters can live upward of five hundred years."

"Wow," Renaldo whispered, nodding. "Right."

Kenny waited silently, uncertain how to move the conversation back to what he wanted. As much as he wanted to ask Renaldo if they were still going to have sex, he couldn't seem to find the words. His cock continued to throb, even with the uncertainty swirling between them, making it a little hard to think.

Evidently, Renaldo didn't seem to have that problem. His human rose to his feet, only to toe off his sandals while whipping his shirt over his head. Then he eased the tips of his thumbs into the waistband of his board shorts.

"So, we'll get to you fucking me," Renaldo stated bluntly.

"Right now. I need to sink my cock into you in the worst way." Tugging his waistband forward, then pushing it down, he revealed his long thick erection, already red and weeping with need. "And I'd be happy for you to bite me and start our bond." Renaldo shoved his shorts down, quickly stepping out of them. "After that, we'll figure out the rest."

Sucking in a sharp breath, Kenny eyed the gorgeous specimen of maleness on display before him. His mate's shoulders were wide, his waist trim, and he had muscles in all the right places. His skin was nicely tanned, with only a bit of tan lines around his groin area, telling Kenny that his mate probably laid out in a speedo.

"Wow," Kenny murmured, admiring Renaldo's large shaft, guessing it to be at least ten inches. Unable to help himself, needing to touch, he reached out and wrapped his fingers around the man's girth. Hearing Renaldo's sharp hiss, Kenny peered up at his mate as he began to slowly jack him. Pleasure filled him upon spotting Renaldo's narrowed eyes and parted lips. His chest expanded and contracted in harsh panting breaths. "You're gorgeous," Kenny praised. "Can't wait to feel this splitting me wide open."

Renaldo growled, his eyes narrowing further. "And I can't wait to do just that." Gently, he gripped Kenny's wrist, stopping his ministrations. "Let's get you undressed. And where's your lube?"

Kenny smirked as he gripped the knot of his towel. "Lube's under the left pillow," he admitted. "Jacked off to memories of you last night." With a deft move, he undid it before flinging it open, revealing that he wore nothing underneath.

Groaning, Renaldo bent and gripped Kenny's hips. "Why are you naked under that towel?" he rumbled even as he easily lifted Kenny and slid him to the middle of the bed. Renaldo followed him onto the comforter. His gaze raked over Kenny

45

in obvious enjoyment. Resting his weight on his left hand, Renaldo skimmed the palm of his right down Kenny's side, across his ribcage, and along his hip. "Been damn near naked all this time."

Panting, tingles erupting over every inch of flesh Renaldo touched, Kenny barely untangled his tongue enough to admit, "Was in the ocean with you." When Renaldo's hand wrapped around Kenny's aching erection and stroked him, he groaned and arched into the touch. "Ren!" he cried, tremors working through him.

Needing more, needing everything, Kenny reached under the pillow and fished out his lube. He held it up, catching Renaldo's attention, pulling it away from where he seemed intent on exploring every inch of Kenny's groin with his firm hand.

For his mate, Kenny wasn't above begging. "Please."

Renaldo pinned him with a feral grin. "Hell, yeah."

Then he grabbed the lube.

CHAPTER SIX

R enaldo knew he should be trying to focus on Kenny's comment — the fact that he'd been swimming in the ocean with them. Except, with all the smooth, olive-toned flesh spread out before him like a buffet, he couldn't concentrate on anything but the beautiful man before him. If Renaldo hadn't known Kenny was a shifter, he would have assumed he was of Italian descent.

Hearing Kenny beg for his touch, to be fucked, drove every last thought out of Renaldo's mind.

Using his thumb, Renaldo popped the cap on the tube. He poured a healthy dollop onto his fingers, then spread it between them to warm the chilly fluid. Renaldo lowered his other hand to Kenny's abdominals and began teasing over his lover's smooth skin.

Renaldo just couldn't seem to get enough of the way Kenny twitched and moaned beneath him. His shifter was just so responsive. He pressed into his palm and arched when Renaldo began to lift his hand, obviously searching for more.

When Renaldo eased his hand between Kenny's legs and touched his wet fingers to his hole, his lover spread his legs even wider invitingly. The move tore a groan from Renaldo's throat, and his erection twitched eagerly. He even felt goose bumps break out over his skin when he eased one finger into Kenny, finally feeling the grip of his hot, tight chute.

"Oh, god," Renaldo muttered gruffly, feeling primed in a way he'd never before experienced. "So fucking good."

"It will be soon," Kenny countered roughly. "More.

Hurry." His dark eyes seemed to glow in the light of the room. "Please, more."

"Hell, yeah," Renaldo agreed, easing a second finger in beside the first. He immediately eased them out, then pushed them back in again, and he marveled at how Kenny seemed to open so easily for him. Moaning at the beauty of his lover's flushed body, nearly ready for him, Renaldo rumbled, "Can't wait."

Kenny bent his knees, planted his feet, and began to rock into each movement of Renaldo's fingers. "Another," his shifter demanded. "I can take it."

For a second, Renaldo paused, uncertain. Then, feeling the muscles around his fingers flutter, he groaned and did as he'd been bidden. He panted roughly as he pressed a third finger in beside the first two, his gut clenching with his arousal.

"You loosen so beautifully," Renaldo mumbled even as he glided the palm of his left hand up Kenny's stomach to his chest. He flicked one nipple, feeling it bead from the simple touch. "God, the way you respond."

"Ren," Kenny mumbled, his hands twisting in the comforter. "G-Gods. Your touch. Amazing." Another moan ripped from him, for right then, Renaldo crooked his fingers and teased over his prostate. "Yesssss!" he hissed through clenched teeth.

Beyond proud to have rendered the much older man to nearly one-word responses, Renaldo chuckled gruffly. He rubbed over Kenny's prostate nearly every pass. At the same time, he tweaked and tugged his nipples. To Renaldo's delight, he watched fluid bubble up from Kenny's slit, pooling quickly, only to begin spilling over the crown.

Renaldo bent, opened his mouth, and stuck out his tongue. Without conscious thought—even though he'd never sucked a cock in his life, he swiped his tongue over Kenny's flared head. He scooped up the nearly translucent pre-cum and moaned softly as the mildly salty flavor burst over his tongue.

Kenny barked Renaldo's name once more, his body shaking in a full-body shudder.

Humming, Renaldo spotted more fluid pooling, so he wrapped his lips around Kenny's crown and suckled lightly. He lost himself in the flavor of his shifter's pre-cum and the exquisite feel of his body wrapped around his fingers. The sound of Kenny's grunts, whines, and groans, coupled with the feel of his lover's flesh beneath his hand, nearly sent his own body up in flames.

"Pleeeease," Kenny whined. "Please, Ren. Please, please, please."

Renaldo popped off Kenny's dick and quickly gripped the base of his erection with his left hand. Groaning, he barely managed to stem his need to come from hearing his lover's cries. Carefully, Renaldo eased his fingers from Kenny's channel as he eyed the flushed male panting before him.

"God, you're so fucking sexy," Renaldo muttered as he grabbed the lube and poured some directly onto his dick. He hissed at the chill, but at least it helped him gain a little control. As Renaldo used his wet hand to spread the slick, he levered over Kenny. "Gonna fuck you into the mattress."

With that vow chanting in his head, Renaldo rested his left forearm on the bed beside Kenny's head. At the same time, he kissed his cock head to his new lover's stretched hole. He pushed experimentally and nearly swallowed his tongue when Kenny opened right up, and his flared crown popped inside, becoming encased in the hottest, tightest heat.

"Oh, fuck," Renaldo whined. It was his turn to shudder, his skin prickling as heat rushed through him.

"Don't stop," Kenny urged, wrapping his arms around his shoulders. He lifted his legs and twined them around Renaldo's waist. Fixing his dark-eyed gaze on him, Kenny began tightening his legs. "Need you, my mate."

Groaning, Renaldo could do little but obey. Between the impressive strength in Kenny's legs coupled with his body's own thrumming need, he couldn't have stopped even if he'd wanted to . . . and he didn't want to.

Renaldo began pushing forward, slowly driving in and in and in. Moving his right hand to Kenny's ass cheek, he hiked his lover's leg higher. He plunged as deeply as possible, burying himself to the hilt.

"Kenny," Renaldo whispered reverently as he stared at where they were joined in the most primitive of ways. His body shuddered as bliss pooled in his groin, making his balls tingle. "So fucking close already."

"Me, too." Kenny whispered the admission.

Renaldo yanked his gaze back to Kenny's face and sucked in a sharp breath upon seeing the desire he saw staring back at him.

"Fuck me," his lover pleaded as he clenched and released his chute muscles around Renaldo's embedded length.

Groaning, Renaldo muttered through gritted teeth, "You top from the bottom."

Kenny suddenly grinned broadly. "Yeah. I'm a power bottom." Waggling his brows, he added, "Just wait until you feel all the things I'm gonna do to your bare dick."

Renaldo moaned even as he began moving. After pulling most of the way out, he reversed direction and plunged back inside. He did it again and again, reveling in the hot grip on his sensitive flesh. Renaldo lost control and slammed into Kenny as swiftly as he was able, over and over, the ecstasy consuming him.

Kenny felt it the second Renaldo lost control and began hammering into him. Feeling his human's erection massage his inner muscles, pegging his prostate every few uncoordinated strokes, he moaned his mate's name. He did his best to rock into each rut and loved that his human ravaged him so completely that he couldn't quite manage it.

Renaldo's taking was raw, primitive, and Kenny's hole sang with the bliss of it.

"Ken!"

Hearing Renaldo shout his name before burying his dick deep inside him and freezing . . . right on his prostate, Kenny moaned as zings zipped up his spine. His balls pulled tight so fast it made his head spin. Before Kenny could even think of controlling himself, his orgasm bowled through him.

Tipping his head back, Kenny joined in his mate's cries as their bodies shuddered and jerked against each other. He clutched at his human's shoulders as he floated on the sweet clouds of ecstasy. The hot warmth of Renaldo's seed registered along with the twitch and pulse of his human's rod lodged within him.

Kenny felt his snake's instinct to claim, to begin their bond, hiss within him. Feeling his teeth extend and sharpen into fangs, he didn't even try to control himself. He turned his head, focused on the meaty flesh where Renaldo's neck met his shoulder, and struck.

As the sweet ambrosia of Renaldo's life-giving fluid oozed up around his fang-like canines, Kenny felt his mate jolt above him. He felt as well as heard him groan. Then the heady iron-rich blood coated his taste buds, and Kenny lost himself in sucking mouthful after mouthful of the exquisite stuff.

Vaguely, Kenny registered the thick rod in his ass twitching within him, telling him that Renaldo had come once more. A second later, his mate's strength seemed to go out, and Kenny found himself with his human's heavy weight pinning him to the bed.

Kenny carefully extracted his teeth. After licking over the bite marks, sealing them and cleaning away all trace of blood, he admired the mark he'd left behind. His sea snake hissed with pleasure upon seeing the gorgeous scar on their mate's neck, and Kenny smiled in agreement.

Relaxing the back of his head on the comforter, Kenny stared at the ceiling. He rubbed his palms over his large human's shoulders and upper back. Tracing over the knobs of his spine absently, he enjoyed the simple pleasure of just getting to touch his human.

Slowing, Kenny traced his way down the strong muscles of Renaldo's back. He reached the crack of his ass and teased at the sensitive skin there. For a second, Renaldo's even breathing stuttered, and Kenny paused.

Once Renaldo was breathing normally again, Kenny couldn't resist skimming his fingertips deeper into his trench. While what he'd told his human was true—he was a power bottom and loved feeling a hard cock pounding away at him—he wanted to claim his mate, too. Kenny couldn't wait for the day when he could feel Renaldo's silky heat wrapped around his long, slender rod, milking him to completion in the sweetest of ways.

Just thinking about it, feeling Renaldo's silky skin beneath his fingertips, caused blood to begin filling Kenny's prick anew. He paused with his fingertips in his mate's trench. His other hand continued to enjoy the feel of his mate's thick back muscles.

One thing could be said for certain. His mate certainly took great care of himself.

"Don't stop there," Renaldo murmured, his warm breath ghosting over Kenny's ear, surprising him that his mate was awake. "I know you want to touch me there."

Kenny hesitated for an instant before asking, "But what about what you want?" Then something else occurred to him. "Have you played with your ass before?"

"No, I haven't," Renaldo admitted. "But don't let that stop

you." With a soft chuckle, he murmured, "From the way you relish every touch, you must think it feels amazing."

Turning his head, Kenny nuzzled his lips against Renaldo's temple. "Yeah. I do," he whispered. "But not all men do."

Renaldo tipped his head to the side and met Kenny's gaze. "And, yet, I won't know until you try." Then he smirked as he rolled his hips a little, reminding Kenny that his human still had his dick in his ass and was still half hard. "What better way to experience it than from this extremely comfortable position?" In an obvious attempt to encourage him, Renaldo spread his legs a bit wider.

Kenny chuckled softly. The move caused his chute muscles to flutter just a bit, and Renaldo moaned in his ear, betraying his enjoyment. Smiling, Kenny began sliding his fingertips farther along his trench, stimulating Renaldo's skin as he moved closer and closer to his objective.

Renaldo hummed, expressing his enjoyment.

Reaching Renaldo's opening, Kenny gently massaged around his ring. He'd played with himself enough times to know what felt good, and he pulled out all the stops. Teasing and rubbing, Kenny worked over what he knew was sensitive flesh.

To Kenny's pleasure, Renaldo moaned softly. "Oh, that's good," he mumbled into Kenny's ear. "Keep doing that." Chucking huskily, he muttered, "Sending a tingle to my balls."

"That's the idea," Kenny assured. "Hang on a sec."

Wanting his mate to enjoy what he intended to do next, Kenny moved his left hand from where he'd been massaging Renaldo's back. After finding the lube, he carefully popped the cap and poured a little on the fingers of his right hand. As Kenny rubbed his fingers together, warming it, he used a thumb to close the tube and set it aside.

Renaldo chuckled softly as he mumbled, "Just felt a few

drips on my back." He pressed a kiss to Kenny's temple. "It's warm enough. Do what you want."

Kenny decided to take Renaldo at his word. Besides, he relished the relaxed, sated scent mixed with renewed arousal emanating from his mate's body. He wanted to know if he could stoke the fires of his human's desire even higher.

Using his thumb in Renaldo's trench, Kenny once again quickly found his mate's hole. He rested his lubed finger on his opening, massaging lightly around it. Once Kenny had it good and wet, he carefully dipped the tip of his forefinger inside the man.

At first, as expected, Kenny felt Renaldo tense, causing his hole to tighten. He wiggled his finger a little, encouraging him to relax. At the same time, Kenny began placing light kisses on his claiming scar.

From the stories told by mated couples, Kenny had heard the claiming scar became an erogenous zone.

Almost immediately, Renaldo grunted and relaxed once more. He sighed deeply, his warm breath causing the hairs on Kenny's neck to stand on end pleasantly. His own prick was once again hard between them, and he barely resisted the desire to rock his hips.

Kenny wanted Renaldo to give in to that need first.

Massaging inside the first couple of inches of Renaldo's body, Kenny slowly worked his mate open. He sought out that pleasure-inducing nub within. While it was a little awkward due to his position, he still managed to find it.

Renaldo moaned softly in Kenny's ear when Kenny first glided over his prostate. His hips twitched, but his chute remained relaxed. When Kenny did it again, then a third time, Renaldo began moving with him, pushing into his ministrations while rutting slowly.

"That's the way, my mate," Kenny murmured into Renaldo's ear. "Take the pleasure I can give you."

"Oh, wow." Renaldo grunted into his ear, his movements becoming surer. With a groan, he whispered, "Doctor's prostate exam, guh, n-never f-felt like th-this."

Kenny had never had a prostate exam, but he couldn't help chuckling at the idea of springing a boner in front of a doctor due to his ass being probed.

Groaning once more, Renaldo shuddered in his arms. When he turned his head and captured Kenny's mouth, he welcomed his mate's tongue. They lapped and nipped, their appendages playing together.

Kenny felt Renaldo's chute tighten around him as his cock jerked in his chute. His mate fed him a groan as a tremble worked through his lover. The knowledge that he'd pleased his human once more caused Kenny's own pleasure to crest. His orgasm swelled through him, and he painted the skin of their stomachs once more.

As Kenny came back to himself, he smiled, appreciating the sucking kisses Renaldo was placing on his neck. If he didn't know better, he would say that his human was leaving a mark of his own.

If he does, I'll wear it with pride.

When Kenny eased his finger free of Renaldo, his human lifted his head and smiled at him, the expression a little loopy. "Wow," he mumbled before letting out a deep sigh. "Much more of that, and I'm sure I'll be begging for your cock in no time."

Chuckling, Kenny took it as a silent challenge.

CHAPTER SEVEN

"So you've agreed to keep it a secret?"

Renaldo sat with his butt against the edge of his desk in his office at work. He'd been surprised to find Elioch waiting in there on Monday morning at eleven. As much as he'd wanted to stay in bed with Kenny all day—repeating the fun from the prior day—Renaldo had followed his usual Monday schedule. He'd risen at eight, and although he'd enjoyed his morning cup of coffee with Kenny on his porch, after that, he'd headed home to get cleaned up and spend a couple of hours in his home office to search for any possible important news reports that he might have missed over the weekend.

He was a firm believer that weekends were not for work. That meant he needed a few hours to play catch-up before starting the week. His line between work and relaxation was extremely important to him.

"As if I had a choice," Elioch replied snarkily. He tapped the side of his head and muttered, "It was either promise or have my memory wiped. Assholes."

With a sigh, Renaldo straightened and began rounding his desk. "Look." Even though the door was closed, he still kept his voice down. "If we're going to live in their world"—Renaldo fought back a wince as he settled in his chair—"then we have to live by their rules."

"Oh my god." Elioch stared at him with wide eyes.

"What?" Renaldo peered up at his buddy in confusion. "What's wrong?"

Elioch snorted even as he grinned broadly. "You totally let

him fuck you."

Renaldo had never made it a habit of sharing particulars with Elioch, and he damn sure wasn't going to start now. Still, there was no point in denying the obvious. Between the mark on his neck—hidden by his tie and suit jacket—and the pain in his ass, it was a little hard for Elioch to miss.

"Kenny claimed me, Elioch," Renaldo told his buddy simply. "We'll leave it at that."

He couldn't help but smile at the memory. By no means would he end up being much of a bottom, not after feeling the full brunt of Kenny's dick inside him, but he would definitely be enjoying finger-play often. Fortunately, he didn't think his shifter lover minded that one little bit, especially not after the number of times Kenny had revved him up and ridden him . . . or begged to be fucked against the wall, over the table, on the bed, in the shower . . .

Renaldo had had more sex in the last forty-eight hours than he had in the last year . . . and he couldn't wait for more.

"Wow, damn."

Upon hearing Elioch's whispered word, Renaldo jerked his attention back to his friend. He saw the man doing a great impersonation of a fish, his mouth opening and closing. Confused once more, Renaldo arched a brow in silent question.

Elioch snapped his mouth shut as he shook his head. "Wow. Never thought I'd actually see the day you'd settle down, but—" His buddy scoffed softly, and his expression turned wistful. "But you really like him. I'm happy for you."

"I do really like him," Renaldo confirmed, nodding. "I'm going to be moving in with him immediately." When he saw Elioch gape again, he lifted his hand, palm out. Still keeping his voice low, he reminded, "It's their way. They find their fated mate, bond, and form a life together. It's weird to think of, sure, but—" Renaldo ran out of words, so he just shrugged.

"Uh, okaaaaaay." Elioch drew the word out before using a

finger to push up his glasses. "People are gonna talk."

Renaldo nodded. "I expect so, which is why I'm going to need your help to spin a believable story." Rubbing the back of his neck, he muttered, "Especially to my mom."

Elioch leaned forward in his chair, resting his forearms on his thighs. "Yeah. Yeah, of course. Anything you want."

Renaldo wondered why Elioch couldn't have given him that response when he'd all but begged his friend to keep his trap shut about the secret of paranormals.

Oh well.

"What do you—" Elioch began, but he was interrupted by the beep of the phone on Renaldo's desk.

Renaldo picked up the handset and lifted it to his ear. "Good morning, Anita," he greeted his secretary.

"Good morning, Mister Martinez," Anita replied back crisply. "I know Mister Parkinson is in there with you, but have you had a chance to review the call receipts I left on your desk, yet?"

"Afraid not," Renaldo admitted, picking up the stack of notes that indicated who had called Friday afternoon and Monday morning. Tucking the handset between his chin and shoulder, he began thumbing through them. "Is there one in particular I need to respond to immediately?"

"Four, actually," Anita told him, surprising him. "Mister Windervine called twice on Friday and twice this morning." For just a second, a hint of annoyance crept into the normally extremely professional woman's voice. "The man seemed to think I was lying each time I said you were out of the office."

Renaldo frowned, finding the four notes she'd stuck together with a paperclip. "Found them." After quickly reading the note that Ramone would like a call back in regards to Perisource's proposal, Renaldo shook his head. "Did he give any indication as to why he wanted to speak to me about the proposal?"

Renaldo was aware that Anita knew he'd already rejected

it.

Anita actually scoffed. "No, sir. I asked, and I quote, *I won't waste my time explaining it to you. Have him call me as soon as possible.*"

"Prick," Renaldo muttered, which earned the smallest of snickers from Anita. He smiled for a second before saying, "I'll call him immediately. Thank you, Anita, and I'm sorry you have to deal with someone like him."

"It's part of the job, Mister Martinez," Anita reminded, calm once again. "What time would you like your break meal to be delivered?"

Anita knew that on Mondays, Renaldo traditionally stayed until five or so, depending on workload. She always asked what time he thought he would need his break. There were several delivery services that she utilized to bring him something to eat and drink, helping to encourage him to take said break.

Some might consider it meddling, but Renaldo appreciated it.

"Actually, my boyfriend is coming to the office around two or so this afternoon," Renaldo revealed. "He'll be bringing me something. Will you show him in when he gets here, please?"

Kenny had explained that newly mated shifters had a hard time being away from their mate for a full day's work . . . at least for a couple of weeks, so Renaldo had asked him to come see him when he took his break. Renaldo truly looked forward to seeing him, too. Even though he'd only left Kenny that morning, he was surprised by how much he already missed him.

"Your boyfriend?"

That was a shocked Anita right there, and Renaldo grinned. "Yes, Anita. My boyfriend. His name is Kenny." He hesitated, realizing he didn't actually know if Kenny had a last name.

Huh.

"W-Wow. Well, color me surprised." Anita chuckled. "I'm very happy for you, sir. It must be serious for you to invite him here."

"Very serious," Renaldo confirmed. *As a heart attack.*

"Well, I'm happy for you," Anita repeated. "I'll send Kenny back as soon as he arrives."

"Thank you, Anita." Then Renaldo placed the handset back in the cradle. He looked up to find Elioch smirking at him. "What?"

"A little playtime during the workday," Elioch teased, waggling his eyebrows. "Kenny must be really, *really* good for you."

Shaking his head at his buddy's antics, Renaldo threw a pen at him.

Not at all coordinated, even though Elioch tried to avoid it, he still got hit on the shoulder. Frowning, he peered at his shirt. "That better not have left a mark."

Renaldo leaned forward, checking his shirt. "Nope. You're good."

When Elioch went to stand, Renaldo lifted his hand and asked, "Why were you waiting in here, anyway?"

Elioch shifted his weight from foot to foot, looking discomfited. "Um." He rubbed the back of his neck. "I, uh . . . I wanted to make sure you turned up on time." After a glance at the wall, Elioch peered at him again with his brows furrowed. "I was worried about you."

"Thanks, man." Renaldo felt truly touched. After all, it was normally him who checked up on Elioch. "I'm good, Eli. Real good." Then he smirked and added, "And if you're all that worried, you could swing over this evening for pizza and beer and help me pack a few things."

Elioch took a step back even as he gaped. "Damn. Moving in tonight?"

"Eh. Sort of." Renaldo waggled his hand in a back-and-forth motion. "Just the essentials so I don't have to keep going home first thing in the morning."

"Wow," Elioch whispered.

Renaldo watched his friend head out the door without another word. While he was a little worried about the man, he turned his attention to work. Picking up the handset, he prepared to make a phone call he was certain would be unpleasant.

After checking the suite number against the board posted in the lobby, Kenny headed toward the bay of elevators. He spotted a man in a suit entering an open door and picked up his pace, calling, "Hold the elevator."

The dark-haired man glanced over his shoulder at him. Curling his lip in a sneer as he looked him up and down, he reached over and punched a button. The doors began to close.

Kenny supposed he could have jogged a few steps and stuck his arm between the doors to make them reopen. He didn't bother, however. After all, then he would have had to deal with the rude man in the elevator.

Instead, Kenny let it go. He ensured the elevator was on its way before hitting the *up* button. Another door opened almost immediately.

Kenny stepped inside and hit the button for the fifth floor. To his surprise, he heard a familiar voice call after him. He placed his hand on the frame and watched Elioch hustle toward him, joining him in the elevator.

Offering Elioch a small smile, Kenny wondered what he should say to the human who'd threatened to expose shifters to the world.

Awkward.

To Kenny's surprise, Elioch stepped close and muttered, "I, uh, I just want to apologize, um, for Saturday." He glanced at him furtively before adding, "Kaiser, um, he showed me some things. Things human hunters have done to, um ... your kind." Elioch whispered the last words while staring at the floor. After a furtive glance up and at the corner, he returned his attention to the floor. "Some people can be real shitheads."

Recognizing Elioch's movements for what they were—he was hiding his lips from the camera and whoever might be in the security office—Kenny followed his lead and also stared at the floor. "It can be a lot to take in, especially when you don't have a mate to smooth the way." After a quick glance at the slender, geeky black man, Kenny added, "Maybe you should join us for our pod barbeques. There are lots of single folks there."

Cocking his head, Elioch asked, "How do you know I'm not seeing someone?"

Kenny tapped the side of his nose. "I'd be able to smell someone else on you."

"Oh." Elioch cleared his throat before saying, "I'll think about it."

"Look, Elioch." Kenny touched the man's upper arm for a second before withdrawing his hand. "You're Renaldo's best friend. I hope, in time, we can become friends, too."

Elioch stared at him, a mixture of surprise and relief in his scent.

It hit Kenny. He'd managed to stumble upon one of the man's concerns. The human feared that Kenny would steal his best friend.

I'll have to make certain to do my best to include this human in any appropriate plans. I'll talk to Renaldo about that.

Finally, as the doors chimed, Elioch smiled at him. "That's nice of you to say."

Before Kenny could reply, the sound of yelling reached his sensitive ears.

"He called me from the office," a man was snarling. "So I know he's here. Don't give me some crap about him not being available. The blinds are open. I can see him through the window, and he's alone and not on the phone."

Kenny hurried around the corner, Elioch on his heels, just in time to see the asshole who hadn't bothered to hold the elevator for him loom over the woman behind the reception desk.

"You announce me, lady, or I'm going to announce myself," he threatened.

"I'm sorry, Mister Windervine," the woman — Anita, according to her name plaque — "but he's already expecting someone. If you would like, I can schedule an appointment for you, and you can come back then."

Pausing ten feet back, Kenny wondered what he should do. The man was obviously a dick, but what if Renaldo was working with him in some way? He didn't want to alienate a client.

To Kenny's relief, Elioch didn't hesitate. "Mister Windervine," he greeted formally as he closed the distance. Kenny couldn't help noticing that he didn't offer his hand. "It sounds like you weren't expected, and Miss Anita is telling you the truth." Elioch indicated Kenny. "Mister Martinez's guest has arrived, so you can either talk with me, or you'll need to schedule an appointment for another day."

Mister Windervine glanced at Kenny and curled his lip again. He opened his mouth, but his attention lingered on the *World of Aquatica* logo on Kenny's polo shirt. Narrowing his eyes, he snapped his mouth shut.

Just then, Kenny's office door opened, and the man in question stepped out. He ignored Mister Windervine in favor of crossing to Kenny. "Hi, babe," he greeted, taking his hand. After lifting it to his mouth and giving his palm a kiss, he smiled warmly at him. "I'm glad you found the place."

"You gave good directions," Kenny replied, doing his best to ignore the elephant in the room. Except, he couldn't. Lowering his voice, he quietly asked, "Do you need a few minutes?"

Renaldo nodded. "Just a minute." Then he turned his attention to the jerk. "Mister Windervine, we said all that needed saying on the phone." Releasing Kenny's hand, he moved that arm to encompass his waist instead. "I must respectfully ask you to leave, or I'll need to call security."

Mister Windervine narrowed his beady dark eyes as he glanced between them. Then, without a word, he pivoted on his heel and stalked out of the lobby.

Once the man was gone, Renaldo shook his head. "Jerk just doesn't know when to accept no." He turned his attention to Anita. "I'm sorry you keep having to deal with that man, Anita." His smile turned wry. "Remind me to give you a raise."

Anita scoffed as she shook her head. "Like I said, it's part of the job." Then her blue eyes glimmered as she added, "But I'll never say no to a raise." Sobering once more, Anita added, "I'll hold your calls."

Renaldo laughed as he began guiding Kenny toward his office. As he passed Elioch, he patted him on the shoulder. "Thanks for the text to get out here, man. I appreciate it."

Elioch nodded, smiling wryly. "You're welcome. Enjoy your . . . meal."

Kenny didn't miss the innuendo in the last word, and evidently, neither did Renaldo. His mate scowled at his buddy while smacking him on the chest with the back of his hand. He then guided Kenny into his office, shutting the door behind them.

After closing the blinds, Renaldo gathered Kenny into his arms and greeted him with a toe-curling kiss.

CHAPTER EIGHT

"I'm really happy for you."

Renaldo glanced up from where he was shutting down his computer. Seeing Anita in the doorway, he smiled. "Thank you. I appreciate that."

He really did, too. It hadn't occurred to him at the time, but there had been a chance that Anita wouldn't have approved of him pairing with a guy. It could have made for an uncomfortable work environment. Either that or she would have quit, and he would have had to go through the trouble of finding another secretary.

And that would have sucked.

"Is there anything you need me to do before I leave?" Anita offered as she always did. "Or first thing in the morning?"

And just as Renaldo always did, he smiled at his secretary and told her, "No, you're so organized, you'd already know if there was."

Anita laughed, as usual, then backed out of the office. "Good night, sir."

Renaldo found himself smiling as he tucked a couple of files into his satchel. He preferred to read possible contracts and proposals on actual paper. That allowed him to rest his eyes in the evening. Too much computer time could get to be a strain.

As Renaldo rested the strap of his satchel over his shoulder, he realized he might not be getting much evening reading done for a while. Smirking, he couldn't say he minded. He exited his office, locking the door behind him. Renaldo did the same to the outer lobby door before heading to the elevator.

Whistling under his breath, Renaldo exited the building out the front door and turned left. He headed toward the nearby parking garage, looking forward to getting home. Renaldo had given Kenny a key to his place during their impromptu late lunch date, and he hoped his shifter would be waiting.

Climbing to the second story of the structure, Renaldo started toward his car. A car stopped before him—a black SUV, and a sensation of déjà vu came over him. Except, when the door opened, it wasn't Alpha Kaiser waiting inside.

Also, the thug in a black suit who got out and pointed a gun at him was definitely not one of the alpha's men.

"Get in, Renaldo," the man inside drawled, a lazy smile on his dark features. "We have some things to discuss."

Renaldo hesitated, wondering if he could get behind a car before the guy with the gun could shoot him. Would he even shoot him? The man in the car seemed to want to talk to him, so that meant he wanted him alive.

"Don't test my patience," the man snapped.

That was when it hit Renaldo. He recognized the man in the car—Armando Whitney, the owner of *Perisource Enterprises*.

Well, shit.

Stepping forward, Renaldo paused in the open doorway as he peered into the vehicle. "Look, Mister Whitney." Perhaps if he proved he knew who the man was, he could get out of this without having to get into the vehicle. "I'm sorry, but I'm not interested in selling or merging. My partner and I like our company's small, family-style vibe."

Armando smirked coldly at him. "I'll consider leaving your little company alone, but you'll need to do something for me, first, Renaldo." His eyes narrowed. "Get in."

Renaldo felt the press of the gun's barrel against his side, and he bit back a groan, knowing he couldn't get out of it. As much as it galled him to do so, he climbed into the SUV and took a seat opposite Armando. To his disconcertion, the guard with the gun climbed in and sat next to Armando.

Someone else closed the door — perhaps the driver — and a moment later, they started on their way.

Maybe I can reach my phone.

I really should have thought of that before . . . or maybe tried to run back down the stairs.

Except, the second Renaldo began lifting his hand to reach inside his jacket, the guard raised the hand holding the gun.

"Put your hands on your lap where I can see them, Renaldo," Armando ordered coldly.

Doing as Armando told him to, Renaldo decided he was done playing nice. "What do you want, Armando?"

Smirking coldly, Armando stated, "I want access to the back section of *World of Aquatica*, and you're going to get it for me."

Renaldo was about to ask why the man would possibly care about that, but a news article slipped into his mind. Armando's son, Braylon, had taken up with someone in security from *World of Aquatica*. He'd ended up being disowned by Armando when he'd moved in with the man.

I bet that man's actually a shifter, and with his request, there has to be far more to the story.

Trying to buy time, Renaldo slowly claimed, "I'm not real familiar with the place. What are you looking for?"

"My son," Armando declared. His smile turned creepy. "And I hear you're dating one of its employees. I'm certain he'll be able to get me where I need to go." Armando's eyes narrowed as he sneered. "For some reason, they're all very protective of their partners. I'm sure that man, Kenny, is it, will do anything to make certain you stay safe . . . including trading Braylon for you." His dark-brown eyes glittering maliciously, Armando ordered, "So, call your little boy toy, and tell him you're ordering a bunch of pizzas. Find a way to convince him to bring Braylon with him. Understood?"

Well, shit.

Hearing his phone ring, Kenny saw his mate's name on the caller ID, and he winced. "I'm sorry I'm running late, Renaldo," he began as soon as he connected the line. "I—"

"Hey, don't worry about it, Kent," Renaldo cut in. "I just left work a few minutes ago, anyway."

Kenny opened his mouth, ready to question the unexpected nickname. He didn't get the chance.

"I'm driving, Kent, so you're on speaker. Don't mind the slight echo," Renaldo continued, his tone sounding a bit off to Kenny. "I'm about to place an order for the half-dozen pizzas we talked about, but I realized I forgot to ask what kind Braylon and Tyrone favor. They're coming, right?" After a second of hesitation, Renaldo added, "I'm really looking forward to seeing them again. What do they like on their pizza?"

In truth, Kenny had no idea what the pair liked on their pizzas. While he knew the big Steller's sea cow shifter in passing—he was part of security at the marine park—they didn't hang out. Kenny opened his mouth, then closed it again.

Okay. I'm so confused.

Instead of admitting that, Kenny decided to roll with it. "Uh, I think Braylon favors the veggie pizza, but he's good picking off any meat he doesn't like," he blatantly lied. "And Tyrone is a fan of the taco pizza."

"Great, I'll add a taco pizza to the order real quick, so I might have to wait a few minutes for them to finish it," Renaldo told him. "I'll text you when I get home, so you're not stuck waiting on the doorstep."

Now Kenny totally knew something was up. He had a key to Renaldo's condo hanging on his keychain. Still, he went along with it.

"Got it," Kenny confirmed. "I don't mind reading a book while waiting. See you soon." After a second of hesitation, he had to add, "Love you. Drive safely."

After a couple of seconds, Renaldo replied softly, "Love you, too, Kenny. See you in a bit."

Shaking his head as the line disconnected, Kenny wished he hadn't shared that news quite like that, but he would never take it back. He quickly called Alpha Kaiser, who picked up on the second ring.

"Please tell me this isn't a problem with Elioch."

"No, Alpha. I don't think we'll have any more problems with him," Kenny replied honestly. "This is about something going on with my mate. He called me, talking about a pizza party, and asked what kind of pizza Tyrone and Braylon like." Even as he heard a low growl come through the line, he quickly added, "Then he made a comment about sitting in my car until he texted, even though I have a key to his place. I'm nearly there, so I plan to have a look around."

"If he's referencing Tyrone and Braylon, I bet it has something to do with the boy's asshole father," Alpha Kaiser declared. "Beta William is in town picking up his mate at the precinct." There was a pause for a heartbeat, then he added, "And Arthur is already calling him. Stay on the line a moment."

"Yes, Alpha," Kenny replied, barely resisting the urge to jam his foot on the accelerator. He couldn't help his mate if he was pulled over for speeding.

Kenny was just pulling up around the corner from the address Renaldo had given him when Alpha Kaiser returned to the line. "According to Ovram, Renaldo's phone is still pinging en route to his house, but the tracker Colton put on his car is still in the parking garage, so he's with someone else."

"Did Colton put a tracker on Elioch's car?" Kenny asked

curiously. He knew the seahorse shifter was the pod's mechanic and kept track of everyone's vehicles.

"Checked that, too," Kaiser revealed. "And it's pinging several miles away, so he's with someone else."

While Kenny didn't understand the first thing about modern technology, the others in his pod did. "Then I have time to get inside before he arrives."

After parking, Kenny pushed from his car and did his best to stride nonchalantly toward the building. There were a number of condos in the ten-story building, so he hoped he just looked like another guy heading home. He also hoped whoever had Renaldo didn't have anyone watching the property.

Considering the hairs on his nape weren't reacting, Kenny felt pretty comfortable. As he walked, he kept his phone to his ear and listed as Alpha Kaiser talked.

"Williams and John are en route with Grisham and Marty. He's a human on the force that John trusts to be discreet," he explained, and Kenny knew the alpha was referring to Marty, not Grisham. Grisham was the police detective mated to Cuzco, a coconut octopus shifter. "Their ETA puts them arriving at almost the same time as your mate and whoever he's with, so Ovram is hacking traffic lights to slow your mate's ride and speed up William's."

"Okay." Kenny didn't know what else to say.

"I also have the doc and his mate en route, just in case their services end up needed," Kaiser added.

"Thank you." While Kenny hoped that wouldn't be the case, he appreciated the sentiment.

By then, Kenny had entered the condo's front lobby. He inhaled discreetly, which told him that Renaldo's scent didn't linger, meaning he hadn't been there in quite some time. While he trusted the ability of those in his pod, his instincts had him checking anyway.

Kenny made it to the eighth floor and found Renaldo's door. Sliding the key into the lock, he opened it easily. He stepped inside, and every sense within him instantly went on alert.

Before Kenny could utter a word, he felt something slam into the side of his head. Had he been human, he knew it would have rendered him unconscious. As it was, the blow caused him to stumble and drop his phone.

His vision spinning, Kenny turned to see his attacker leaping toward him again. The man wore a black suit and screamed of malicious intent. Fortunately, he was the only one whose scent mixed with the sweet goodness of his mate's, telling him the guard must have been a lookout, and he was alone there.

Kenny easily evaded the human's second attack. Spinning so he was behind him, he grabbed the human's shoulders and yanked him close. Dropping his snake's fangs, he leaned forward, stabbed them into the taller man's lower shoulder, and pumped the venom from his glands into the man's body.

The human froze for all of two seconds before his body bowed with pain, and his scream rent the air.

Undeterred, Kenny poured a second shot of venom into the large human. He felt the man convulse and quickly pulled his fangs free. Releasing the guy, Kenny wiped the back of his sleeve across his mouth as he took a step backward and watched him fall to the floor.

After one more convulsion, the man slipped into unconsciousness.

Kenny arched his neck and retracted his fangs. After a rub to his temple, he crossed the floor and found his dropped phone. He heard his alpha's holler before he even managed to bring it to his ear.

"I'm here, Alpha," Kenny stated gruffly. "I'll be okay.

There was a lookout waiting here." After a second of hesitation, he knew he had to come clean. "If the doc has already left and he doesn't have any anti-venom on him, then you need to have someone bring it asap."

"Shit," Alpha Kaiser muttered. "How'd you shift to snake and back so fast?"

"I didn't," Kenny admitted, wanting to find some water so he could wash his mouth out. "I don't need to shift to drop my fangs and inject venom."

"Well, fuck, Kenny," Kaiser murmured, sounding shocked—which was a first for Kenny to hear. "Why the hell do you go through milking then?"

Kenny sighed deeply before admitting, "Species secret. It's been known to freak out other shifters, and we've been kicked out because of it."

"Well, that won't happen here," Kaiser assured. "I'll want—"

Just then, a woman knocked on the still cracked door. "Is everything okay?" she asked, peering at him through the crack and starting to push open the door. "I thought I heard a scream."

"You did, ma'am," Kenny replied honestly. It wasn't as if he could hide the bruiser on the floor swiftly enough. "My buddy slipped and hit his head." Wiggling his cell phone, Kenny lied, "Paramedics are already en route."

"Oh, will he be okay?" She looked like she wanted to drop to the floor and check him, which Kenny couldn't allow.

"I hope so," Kenny decided to go with. "I'll—" He spotted movement over her shoulder and relief flooded him. Beta William and Captain John Casinov approached. "Thank you so much for coming." He cast a quick glance toward the woman, before focusing on the beta. "My buddy hit his head. Are the paramedics on their way up?"

Beta William caught on fast. "They sure are." Then the

dominant shifter turned his charm on the woman, getting her to move on quickly.

The police captain stepped close to Kenny and murmured, "What happened to him?"

"Attacked me when I entered, so I neutralized him," Kenny replied.

Captain Casinov nodded, even as his phone chimed. He pulled it from the holder on his belt and looked at it. Then his lips curved into a wide smile, and he focused on Kenny.

"Good news. Detectives Grisham and Marty, along with a little help from the building's security guards, have apprehended Armando Whitney and his three goons." His smile widened into a grin. "Your man is nailing them with kidnapping charges. I can't wait to finally put that asshole behind bars."

"And Renaldo?" Kenny pressed, taking a step toward the door. "Is he safe?"

"I sure am," Renaldo appeared from around the corner, coming into the room. Sporting a large, relieved-looking smile as he eyed Kenny, he spread his arms wide. "Thanks to you, my shifter."

Kenny quickly accepted the invitation and stepped close, folding his human into a hug of his own. "Anything for you," he murmured roughly, so very happy to have his mate back in his arms, safe and sound. At least, Kenny hoped he was. "Are you okay?" he asked, rubbing up and down Renaldo's back. "Are you injured? Doc Anthony is on his way."

"I'm just fine," Renaldo assured before tightening his hold, dipping his head, and claiming Kenny's mouth.

Kenny opened instantly to Renaldo, accepting his mate's appendage. Flicking out his own tongue, he did a little tasting of his own as they ravaged each other's mouths.

Absently, Kenny felt someone tug his phone from his grip, but he didn't care. He had what he wanted, what he needed, tucked safely in his arms. He also heard Beta William laugh and say something about taking care of the guy on the floor *in house*. Kenny knew that meant the guy would be treated for venom, his mind altered, and he would eventually be released.

That didn't matter either, because right then, Renaldo palmed Kenny's ass and lifted.

Kenny spread his legs and wrapped them around Renaldo's waist. He felt the world spin—perhaps more than normal with his head still ringing a smidge—but he didn't care. Kenny had everything his heart could ever need. His mate carried him through his house, although Kenny was too busy kissing him back to look around.

When Kenny's back hit a mattress, he finally focused on his mate long enough to say, "I love you, Renaldo."

With a warm smile lighting his brown eyes, Renaldo replied, "And I love you, my shifter."

After that, nothing else mattered as Kenny lost himself in his lover's claiming. Soon, he intended to inspect every inch of his mate's body . . . all night long . . . but right then, Kenny was more than happy to let Renaldo have his way.

ABOUT THE AUTHOR

Charlie started writing fantasy when she was eight, and after stumbling onto her first erotic romance at age nineteen, she realized her true calling. She now focuses on writing gay erotic romance, normally of the paranormal variety, with heroes of all kinds. With the help and support of her husband, Charlie finally fulfilled one of her life-long goals . . . move to acreage with her horses. You can often find her curled up with her laptop and a cup of tea or glass of wine, creating her next adventure. Charlie enjoys exploring the mountains of her new Oregon home on horseback, 4-wheeler, or motorcycle.

She can be reached at ch.richards2010@yahoo.com

Or visit her at www.charlie-richards.com.

www.ingramcontent.com/pod-product-compliance
Lightning Source LLC
Chambersburg PA
CBHW070540130626
46555CB00003B/1507